SAPPHIRE BLUE

Other books by DeAnn Smallwood:

Montana Star

SAPPHIRE BLUE
•
DeAnn Smallwood

AVALON BOOKS
NEW YORK

Published by Thomas Bouregy & Co., Inc.
160 Madison Avenue, New York, NY 10016

Library of Congress Cataloging-in-Publication Data

Smallwood, DeAnn.
  Sapphire blue / DeAnn Smallwood.
     p. cm.
  ISBN 978-0-8034-9956-0
  1. Women healers—Fiction.   2. Montana—Fiction.   I. Title.

PS3619.M358S37 2009
813'.6—dc22

                                                    2008052527

PRINTED IN THE UNITED STATES OF AMERICA
ON ACID-FREE PAPER
BY HADDON CRAFTSMEN, BLOOMSBURG, PENNSYLVANIA

To my husband Marvin, my best friend,
who never complains about my preoccupation
when I live in my writer's world. I truly bask
in your pride as you place my books in
a prominent spot in our living room.
How did I ever catch you?

A very special acknowledgement and thank you to Janet Zupan, editor, writer, and friend. You have such a gift of knowing when I need to be reassured. My books simply would not be without your insight, editing ability, and encouragement. You wear many hats for me. You are a Sapphire!

Thank you to writer and friend, Robert Lee, for unselfishly sharing Janet. A novice asked, and you came through.

Chapter One

From her riotous red curls to the tips of her toes, Meghan O'Reiley knew that life was unfair. She told herself it didn't matter. *Witch* was the whispered name they called her. *Strange* was another, kinder one.

She knew that when a hesitant knock came on her cabin door, it would be a birthing, a sickness, or an accident that demanded her presence.

When Granny was alive, she'd done most of the nursing. But Granny had been dead three years now. Meghan still mourned her. Not just because of the security she had offered, but because she deeply loved the old woman, like the mother she'd never known.

Meghan brushed a rebellious curl that had escaped the bandana she wore when mixing her remedies. "Witch," she muttered under her breath. "As if this is magic and not work, all the gathering, drying, storing, and bundling herbs. As if it doesn't take special knowledge and training to know what to mix together to heal sicknesses."

The sun bounced off the mica-speckled boulders sheltering the back of the cabin and through the four small windowpanes of the clean kitchen. The beams lit on the errant curl, adding another facet of fire to it. Had not the remainder of thick curls and waves been subdued by the kerchief, they, too, would be flashing a golden red light as they tumbled freely around her face and down her back. Like their owner, the thick curls had a will and independent streak of their own.

The smell of sage filled the kitchen, growing more redolent as the leaves were angrily crushed under the wooden pestle in the hardwood bowl.

"Need something for Davy's hoarseness," the woman from the valley had said.

"Ha!" Meghan snorted, a scowl marring her pixie face. "Hoarse, is he? Well, no wonder. I'd like to tell that mother of his that her precious Davy led two other boys in pelting me with pinecones all the way up the mountain yesterday. Following me home, running and jumping out from behind trees, yelling like banshees. I'm glad he's hoarse," she said peevishly. Then she was filled with guilt over her thoughts. Rarely was she given to negative feelings, but yesterday's events were still churning inside her. "Quit feeling sorry for yourself, Meghan O'Reiley," she remonstrated. "The majority of the valley folks are grateful and appreciate all I can do for them."

The only response was the snap of the kindling where

it burned in the belly of the cookstove. The fire and the cheerful hiss of the big iron teakettle filled the kitchen with a coziness that Meghan momentarily overlooked, so intent was she on her thoughts.

Sadness suddenly overwhelmed her, and she angrily rubbed the side of her face against a raised shoulder, brushing away the tears that filled her eyes.

"Oh, Granny, I miss you so. I know you've gone to a better place, but darn it to heck and back," she muttered, "you left me. You left without answering all my questions, and . . . and you left me alone."

"Kid." Granny's soft voice filled the kitchen. *"Kid, you can do anything you set your mind to. Why, you could take care of these poor fools standin' on your head."*

A tentative smile touched Meghan's lips as she imagined the short, stout woman. She could see Granny's faded apron pulled tightly across her ample breasts and tied around her thick waist. Granny, hands never idle. She often challenged Meghan by using her favorite expression, *"Why, you could do . . . standin' on your head,"* filling in with whatever it was she wanted Meghan to do or think about. Granny, whose lap was ample enough to cradle a little girl through the knocks and bumps of growing up. And always, Granny who took the brunt of the towns folk's hurtful words, explaining them away as proof of some people's ignorance.

Those memories now filled Meghan with the quiet determination instilled in her by the woman she'd known only as "Granny." From the moment she'd opened her cabin door to find baby Meghan, wrapped in a dirty piece of fur, lying on her doorstep, Granny had dispensed lessons on facing the world and all it had to throw at you, determinedly.

Baby Meghan hadn't cried. In fact, as Granny was later to tell her with a fond chuckle in her voice, she'd almost stepped on her lying there, *"having yourself a fine conversation with those fists you was wavin' about."* When Granny had peeled off the wet piece of fur, she'd found a scrap of paper with something scrawled on it. *Name's Meghan O'Reiley. Don't want no baby.* Two lines, no more. Well, Granny had wanted her. She'd scooped up the infant and taken her inside the cabin, where Meghan grew up happy and secure in Granny's love. Happy with their secluded life interrupted only by the demands of the townspeople living below.

A town had sprung up around a few gold mines after the discovery that the blue rocks the miners had previously tossed out of their gold pans were worth something after all. There were several Yogo sapphire mines throughout the Judith Valley. Some were owned by the English. The mine in Pig Eye Gulch was smaller than most, and Meghan wasn't sure who owned it. History on the Yogo sapphire was scant, but it gave Meghan insight as to why this precious stone was now being held in higher regard. *Yogo* was an Indian word meaning blue stone, and the *saphyre*, as it was first called, was thought by early physicians to have curative powers. It would be ground into powder and used to make salves to heal sores, pustules, and boils. It was also thought that rubbing the blue stone on a tumor would heal it.

The miners' families needed Granny's vast knowledge of herbs and healing, knowledge that she meticulously taught and joyfully passed on to Meghan. It was a knowledge as old as the hills—of the plants, roots, and berries that grew around them in plentiful supply in this Montana valley.

"Equal parts powdered licorice and calamus. Mix with honey and take one teaspoon three to four times daily. Warm the body with a sage tea (four parts), black pepper (a pinch), cinnamon (one half part)." Meghan could recite the mixture by heart, just as she could hundreds of others. Granny had written down many of the decoctions and instructions, but Meghan rarely referred to the spidery scrawls anymore. She had committed the recipes to memory, easily matching the ailment with the cure, putting herbs and instructions into a canvas bag sewn on the old treadle machine.

She took one step out the door, glanced down at her bare feet, and turned back inside. "Meghan," she admonished herself, imitating Granny's voice, "don't you dare go outside in those bare feet. It's gettin' on to fall now, and I don't have the time to be doctorin' an ailin' young'un." She smiled to herself as she parroted the oft-told reminder to a young girl who hated to give up the summer warmth for hateful shoes that she would be forced to wear until spring returned.

Meghan pulled out her high golden moccasins and tied the rawhide thongs, securing them to her ankles. She rubbed the soft elk skin and silently thanked Granny.

She'd been all of four years old when Granny had come up with the glorious compromise of moccasins to replace the detested shoes. The hides were purchased from a miner. Granny sat down to the old treadle and followed a pattern she'd traced from a pair of Meghan's shoes, trimming and folding the hide. Each pair got better until both Granny and Meghan became adept at fashioning the footwear.

Summer brought out a pair of soft-slip ons used for those occasions when they went into town or when rain brought a chill to the valley. Winter brought forth a pair with the perfectly tanned hide on the outside and merino wool on the inside. The merino came from their very own sheep. Sheep that Granny sheared each year, before washing and carding the soft wool fibers, later spinning them into yarn for sweaters, with always enough set aside for the lining of Meghan's moccasins.

Granny had taught Meghan the art of spinning. Meghan had chased and played with the hardy, white-faced sheep that Granny had told her came all the way from Italy. Granny had bought a male and a female from a miner down on his luck. Each year the pair presented them with one, and on rare occasions two, offspring. The little herd would grow in number until Granny would get a man to kill the oldest, feeblest one. They'd cook the tough mutton, using the fat as waterproofing on their shoes and moccasins and as a prime ingredient in a soothing rub that gave relief to many a chest cold and complaint.

Although Granny never could bring herself to do the

killing, she instilled in Meghan the importance of recognizing life's natural cycle and of making the most of its necessary end.

"We only kill what we need to eat, Meghan," she taught her. *"And then we make sure we use every bit. We don't waste what God has given us. There's a time for everything. Recognizing the end of our time is just as important as livin' each and every minute we're given."*

Meghan followed that same principle but found it hard even to cull her flock of chickens. As a child Meghan had to hunt out some of the broody hens and run them off their nests, or she'd have them all setting, hatching out more chicks than they wanted. She glanced down at a small scar on her right hand, close to her thumb, where a determined hen had given the young Meghan a good peck as she'd tried to reach in under her to steal her eggs to discourage her from setting on them. Meghan had run bleeding to Granny to have the small wound patched up and to receive another lesson on life.

"Nothin's stronger than a mother's need to protect her young'un, kid," she said, using her pet name for Meghan, *"and that old hen sees them eggs as her young'uns."* After that, Meghan used more patience and showed more respect for the broody hens.

"In a pinch, kid, you've only got yourself to depend on. Don't look to others for your needs, or you'll be disappointed. Learn to like yourself, Meghan. You're the best friend you got."

And she did, taking Granny's lessons to heart. Granny would sell the eggs and extra vegetables to the general store in town, where they would be eagerly purchased by the miners and their families. What happened to the money that passed from the storekeeper's hand to Granny's, Meghan never knew or cared. Money had no place in her small, secure world. No place at all until that hateful fall day when Granny sat her down at the kitchen table, covered with a flowered oilcloth faded from many washings, and put out a cup of peppermint tea and a plate of homemade butter cookies.

Meghan knew instantly there was something Granny wanted to teach her. The kitchen table had been the setting for many such meetings. Still, she was totally unprepared for the announcement. She sat down and eagerly reached for one of the still-warm cookies. She knew well enough by now that Granny would adhere to her philosophy that nothing was so bad to discuss, no situation so severe, that it couldn't be talked out over a cup of tea and a plate of cookies hot out of the oven or a slice of homemade bread with jam.

But Granny's philosophy didn't work this time. This time Granny was wrong. What she had called Meghan in to discuss was so bad that no amount of tea or fresh-baked cookies would help.

"Meghan," Granny had begun, *"you'll be sixteen in a few short weeks."* Meghan nodded her head in agreement. Gone was the skinny, knobby-kneed girl, and in her place was a beautiful young lady showing signs of becoming a graceful woman. Meghan was already taller than Granny. She differed from Granny in shape also. Where Granny was short and stout, Meghan was willowy with a narrow

waist. Her skin was creamy, enhanced by a sprinkling of freckles. But it was her mass of hair that was indeed her crowning glory. It invited a touch to see if it was as fiery as it looked. It invited crushing in your hand to see if it would rebel and spring back as full of curls and bounce as ever.

Granny never hesitated to tell Meghan how pretty she was. She didn't believe it would do any harm for the child to grow up enjoying this knowledge. Yet she told her in such a way that young Meghan accepted the fact without letting it rule her head. What was more important to Meghan than words about her beauty were words of praise for a task well done, or the pride in Granny's voice and eyes when Meghan had done something kind and caring. Right or wrong, she was supported in standing tall for herself and whatever she felt was right and fair. The only reprimand she ever received was when she let her fiery temper rule her mouth and actions.

Meghan had waited for Granny to continue.

"You've done well in your studies. Mrs. Highback is very pleased with the lessons we send her. Guess we didn't do too bad on the schoolin', kid." Mrs. Highback was a friend of Granny's who lived in Great Falls, Montana. Meghan had never been to the city, but Granny kept in touch with her friend by mail.

Meghan had turned seven when Granny decided Meghan needed some formal schooling. There had never been a question of her going into the town in the lower part of Pig Eye Gulch; it was too far for a little girl. And in the same way that the folks there weren't fond of their children's associating with her, Granny wasn't willing to have Meghan exposed to them. Mrs. Highback was a teacher, and soon the first of many packages of books and lesson plans arrived from Great Falls bearing her return address.

A determined Granny opened the first package, read through the lesson plans the night before, and the next morning set down the law for a reluctant Meghan. School would be every day, Saturday and Sunday alike. It would be for four hours a day, sitting at the kitchen table under Granny's tutelage, and then a few more hours on Meghan's own, reading or studying an assignment. Granny would tolerate no variance in this law. If something called Granny from the cabin either for a few hours or a few days, Meghan was expected to continue as though Granny was sitting in the chair opposite her at the table. Granny would not raise an ignorant child.

In time, Meghan came to look forward to the assignments almost as much as she looked forward to her lessons in cooking, cleaning, sewing, keeping a home, and—her favorite lessons of all—healing and caring for the sick. Meghan absorbed everything like a little sponge. Mrs. Highback was delighted and answered the challenge by sending more advanced work.

"Well, we've done all we can do. Mrs. Highback says you've went beyond what she can help us with and that you need more formal schoolin'."

Meghan had sat up straighter, and a chill crept up her spine. Suddenly she was afraid.

*"Meghan, you're growin' up too fast on me. I can't be selfish and keep you here with an old lady and a few sheep for company. You need to meet other girls your own age. You need—*and Granny's voice broke and lowered— *"You need to be exposed to the world, kid. Now, don't interrupt me, Meghan. Let me say what I gotta. I been studyin' on this long enough, and I know we got to do this."* Granny took a deep breath. *"I'm sending you into Great Falls, where you will be attendin' Amy Fairchild's Academy for Young Women. It's a good school, accordin' to Mrs. Highback. You'll board there, but you can come back here summers and vacations."*

"Don't you want me anymore, Granny?" Meghan had asked softly, her voice full of the hurt and fear that had clutched her heart at Granny's words.

"Land's sake, child, of course I want you. You're my life's breath. This is your home, Meghan O'Reiley, and will be for as long as you want it. But, this is best, kid. I wouldn't give you up for a second if I didn't think so."

And so it was done. No amount of protesting or begging worked. And just shy of her sixteenth birthday, Meghan caught the weekly mail stage for Great Falls. Two days later she sat on the edge of a straight-backed chair across the desk from the forbidding Amy Fairchild, whose pursed, thin lips spelled out the rules and expectations of anyone lucky enough to be accepted into Amy Fairchild's Academy for Young Women.

Meghan hated every minute of it. She hated the restrictions and many rules that seemed to have no reason. She was ostracized by the other genteel young ladies who made fun of her country ways, her ignorance of social graces, her lack of social standing, and her homemade clothes. Oddly, though, they were also jealous of her knowledge that was far superior to theirs, and her beauty that seemed to grow as Meghan matured. She never spoke of this to Granny, nor did she share how miserable she was at Amy Fairchild's. She didn't question where the money came from to send her to this prestigious school, but she knew it had to be expensive, and if Granny was making that sacrifice, then she darn well could take whatever Miss Fairchild and the young ladies could dish out. She owed it to Granny to make the most of every minute spent there, and if it was spent with a lump of homesickness in the pit of her stomach, so be it. She lived for every summer and holiday, and if Granny looked more tired and older with each visit, it was because Meghan missed her so much, she was probably imagining it.

She'd been an unwilling and largely unwelcome student at Amy Fairchild's Academy for close to two years when one chill morning Miss Fairchild called her in and bluntly informed her of Granny's death. With the coldly delivered news came an unopened letter from an attorney in Great Falls. Miss Fairchild handed it over, pursed her lips disapprovingly, and waited for Meghan to tell her the contents.

Meghan quickly scanned the document, then slowly read it again. As she read it the second time, she realized she held freedom in her hands. She glanced up at the stern face and cold eyes watching her and knew they no longer held any threat nor offered any comfort for her pain and loss. Granny's death had released Meghan from any obligation to stay here and try to please Miss Fairchild, a woman incapable of being pleased.

"I will be leaving within the hour, Miss Fairchild." The words were delivered not by an intimidated schoolgirl but by a young woman who, from the tilt of her chin and the set of her shoulders, was now a woman to be reckoned with.

"The letter, please, Miss O'Reiley." Miss Fairchild stretched forth her hand.

"The letter is personal, Miss Fairchild. It is not your concern. As I said, I will be leaving within the hour. However, there is a prepaid balance of my tuition for the remainder of the year. I do not expect to be reimbursed for the balance of this month, but I will require the payment made for the forthcoming three months." And with that, Meghan held forth *her* hand.

"Well, I . . . I never! I've never had money demanded in such a crass, undignified manner. Indeed, the act says it all, Meghan O'Reiley. I feel your years here have done little to form and polish your—" She was interrupted just as she was warming to yet another belittling comment.

"Miss Fairchild, I have spent almost two years here listening to you find fault with everything about me. If it wasn't my hair, it was my lineage or lack thereof. I tolerated it because I owed it to my granny. With her death, that debt is canceled." Meghan rose from the chair, unconscious grace in every movement. She leaned toward

Miss Fairchild, causing an involuntary recoil from the astonished woman, whose mouth opened to a small *o*.

"I will stop by this office to retrieve the entire sum due me in one hour." Meghan turned and walked out of the office and, with head held high, went back to her impersonal room to pack. Granny was gone. But she would not mourn her in this hateful place. She would save that until she reached her beloved home at the base of the Big Snowy Mountains. She would not read again the Last Will and Testament until she was seated at the oilcloth-covered table in the warm kitchen filled with Granny's spirit. Then, and only then, would Meghan mourn.

Chapter Two

Meghan shook her head to clear it of the memories and of Granny's voice, which came back to her often. Shoes on, she closed the door behind her and stood on the small porch, breathing in the fresh mountain air tinged with the smoke from her woodstove and with the early bite of fall.

I'm lonesome. The unbidden thought came as she walked down the path from her house. She never mentioned a fee for her services, knowing that for all their mean-spirited taunts and comments, the great pride each person in this valley had would make them pay her adequately for her knowledge and time. Those who didn't have cash would pay with whatever means they could. Sometimes it was split wood for her stove, sometimes it was something homemade, and sometimes it was a small pouch of gold mixed with a few of the blue stones that washed out of the gulch. She appreciated it all equally.

The money and gold pouches she put in a jar and buried in the small chicken house, as granny had, leaving then, deposits in her Will. Meghan had smiled the first time she dug in the area described in Granny's letter. Only her wise, practical, Granny would think of burying the money jars in such an undesirable place. They were safe for sure—Meghan chuckled—under the litter of chicken droppings and feathers. Meghan suspected that Granny had picked this spot with great pleasure. Meghan never counted how much money was buried there, but she now assumed that this was where her school tuition had come from. Then, after she'd been home for about six months, she found out otherwise.

It was in the spring, following her first winter alone. She had the door to the cabin open to let in the morning sunshine, when she heard a donkey's bray. Expecting to see someone from the town needing her services, she looked up from where she spaded the loamy ground of her garden. A tall, skinny man sporting a winter's growth of beard sat astride a mule. There was a scowl on his face. His eyes moved away from her and up the path to the open door of the cabin, then back to Meghan. Then he slid off the mule, looped the lead rope—connected to another donkey loaded with packs and camp goods—around the pommel of the worn saddle, and, still peering at her through squinted eyes, walked toward her.

Meghan's heart raced, and she wished she'd grabbed

the shotgun by the door. She was a good shot—Granny had seen to that—but a fat lot of good that would do her now. The scowling, whiskered man would be on her before she was halfway to the door. Gulping down her fear, she decided to bluff her way out of the frightening situation.

"What do you want?" she asked with as much bravado as possible.

"Where's the old woman?"

Involuntarily Meghan looked at the small knoll where a picket fence enclosed a carefully tended piece of ground.

The man's eyes followed hers. He gave a slight nod, then said, "You kin?"

"Granddaughter," Meghan said quietly.

"Good enough." He held out the saddlebag he'd slung over one shoulder. "This here's all she lent me." With that he laid the saddlebag on the ground at Meghan's feet and turned away.

"Wait!" Meghan called out. "I don't understand. What do you mean, she lent you?"

The man turned back to her. "Your grandma was a good woman." He made the comment as if daring anyone to challenge it. "About a year ago, I was down on my luck. I made it as far as this town. Hadn't ate for a spell and sure didn't know when I would next, so I went into the general store and asked the owner if he'd grubstake me for a fifty-fifty split of any gold I'd find. I weren't askin' for charity. A grubstake's different." The man's eyes turned hard, and he spat a stream of brown juice into some weeds, then wiped his mouth with the back of one hand. "The storekeep didn't want no part of me or my offer. In fact, he didn't want me in his store."

He took a deep breath and turned away from Meghan, looking into the distance. "I was standin' there in the dust, wonderin' which way to go, when I heard a voice. 'You like rabbit stew?' Dang near fell over in a dead faint just thinkin' about it." He gave a hoarse laugh. "This old lady was lookin' at me, peerin' right through me. 'I sure do,' I said. 'Then come with me.' She jerked her head toward the woods, and I followed right behind her. Pret' near didn't make it, I was so weak. She led me right up to this cabin, opened her door, and motioned me inside. I ken tell you now, the smell darn near did me in. She took down a bowl and filled it, then unwrapped dishtowel from around a loaf of bread and began slicing."

He turned back to Meghan, who could see the scene in her mind, recognizing Granny's every movement. "Well, lady, I can tell you now, I ain't never eat nothin' as good as that rabbit stew. I ate me several bowls and half that loaf of bread. She sat there, sippin' a cup of coffee, and never said a word until I pushed the bowl away for the last time. Then she said, 'Tell me about needing a grubstake.' So I told her 'bout how I'd found gold up in"—he paused—"uh, up in one of the draws. I marked the spot and left for the valley, where I planned to buy me some supplies so's I could winter up there."

He stopped speaking. When he resumed, his voice was low. "I never made it to the valley. Outside Lewistown, my horse shied at a fresh bear track and throwed me. I struck my head on a rock and didn't know anythin' else until I woke up a week later in a shack behind a blacksmith's shop. Took me a couple more weeks to get my feet back under me. My horse had taken off for parts unknown, along with my saddlebags with all my belongin's and what little cash I had. I stayed there until spring, then caught a ride on a wagon heading toward Great Falls. I left it partway and took off on foot to here. Don't mind sayin' that by the time your grandma came on me, I was pretty well done in. What strength I'd gained back was nigh on gone from hunger."

"Your grandma made me up a mat on the floor, and for the next few days she fed me and let me sleep. We talked some each day about the grubstake and the gold I'd found. 'You sure you can find it again?' she'd ask me. 'Yep,' I'd tell her, 'I darn well know I can.'

Then one morning she handed me two jars. One had cash money rolled up inside of it, and the other had a pouch of gold. She told me it was my grubstake. I was to go back to town and buy me a horse and whatever supplies I needed to get me through the winter, and get me that gold. I told her the same as I told that storekeeper, fifty-fifty. She shook her head and told me just to bring back what money she'd given me. She said that she needed it for a granddaughter in a fancy school in Great Falls. She gave me a sassy grin and told me that, of course, if I wanted to throw in a little extra, she wouldn't turn her back on it.

Well"—he rubbed a grimy hand across his beard—"I took her money. Tried to thank her, but she wouldn't hear of it. She told me I wasn't the first prospector she'd grubstaked, and I wouldn't be the last. Said she trusted me 'cause she hadn't ever been took by any one of us."

He stopped talking, and the silence of the pines closed around them. He turned and walked back to the mule. Once on its back, he unwound the rope from the saddle horn and looked back at Meghan. "That saddlebag's got what I owed her." He turned the mule back onto the path leading toward the town. His next words drifted back over his shoulder. "An' a little extra."

Chapter Three

Meghan sighed as she looked across the valley. The sun was setting earlier each day. Meghan never tired of the changing seasons, the view from her kitchen window or the front porch offering a panoramic view of them and of the valley below. She took a sip of coffee, watching the thin curl of steam rise into the cool morning air.

The peace of the mountains entered her, and she smiled. Yesterday had been a day of remembering. But today was a day to bask in the glory of the master artist. Each bush had a color of its own, and they all blended together perfectly. A tree at the edge of the woods dropped a small leaf, and Meghan watched it spiral and twist to the earth. It would soon be forgotten under the snow that would cover the Big Snowy Mountains and the valley below. She took another sip of coffee and sighed contentedly. She knew the temperature would rise to the fifties or sixties today, and she'd have yet another perfect Montana autumn day.

"Enjoy but work, Meghan O'Reiley. You have lots to do before the snow falls and only a few short months to do it. Meghan grinned at the reproachful voice in her head, but still she didn't move from her spot. A squirrel scampered from behind a tree at the edge of the clearing. It stopped and raised itself upright, its snappy eyes quickly surveying the area. With tiny ears pitched forward and nose wiggling, every muscle alert, it was ready to spring back into the safety of the trees should danger appear. Meghan was still. She knew the squirrel saw her, but the pieces of corn she'd scattered at the edge of the clearing were too great a temptation to resist. Especially with winter coming on.

Reluctantly, Meghan turned her back on the autumn splendor. She closed the door to the cabin and, setting her coffee cup in the dishpan, started her morning chores. She was going to pick some of the smaller cucumbers to make sweet pickles. She would have to go out to the shed behind the cabin and bring in a couple of crocks to set up the cucumbers in a brine that would have to be changed and added to over the next fourteen days. The cabin would soon be redolent with the pleasant smell of heated spices. What she didn't save for her own use, Meghan would take into town to be traded for staples.

Autumn meant canning and a sense of urgency to prepare for the winter months ahead. Meghan thought of the empty jars lining the shelves of the storage shed. Those would have to be brought in and washed before she could begin the canning. She'd had a bigger than usual garden this year, and she'd learned long ago that to waste anything, especially food, was wrong.

The coming days would be busy, but thanks to Mr. John Mason's glass jar, canning was a lot easier for Meghan than it had been when Granny was young.

Meghan had learned the cold-packing method from hours of standing on a small stool beside Granny, helping her process jar after jar of vegetables and fruit, sealing each one with a glass lid. It had been Meghan's job to heat the rubber rings in a pan of boiling water. Then, when Granny had filled the jar, Meghan would place the hot ring on it, take the glass lid, and place it on the ring. Her nimble fingers then fit the metal bail firmly over the lid.

With Meghan becoming more help than hindrance with each passing year, the canning was accomplished with ease and the pleasure of working together in the cozy kitchen. The heat of the boiling water and the aches in their backs from hours of standing, peeling, and lifting went almost unnoticed as they laughed and shared the hard work. After it was all done, Granny and Meghan would open the door of the root cellar and admire the rows of shiny jars filled with vegetables, meat, small potatoes, pickles, fruit, and sweet, succulent jellies and jams. They felt a wealth that couldn't be measured in money. They were ready for the winter and all it could throw at them.

Next to canned, goods were containers holding their

precious spices, and herbs hung drying from the rafters. The herbs held healing secrets known to Meghan and Granny, and the preserved food and medicinal herbs, held equal value and importance to the two women.

Meghan thought of the job ahead of her and knew it would start with today's pickles. Each year she promised herself she'd take some of her money and buy one of the fancy pressure canners developed by Mr. Shriver to ease the task ahead. But so far she hadn't done it. Maybe this year. It sure would be faster, and with her garden harvest being so large . . . But Meghan knew she wouldn't. It seemed a frivolous use of money, an indulgence she wasn't used to. She knew she needed some warm material for shirts and pants to get her through the cold winter months, and that would take enough of her money. Warm clothing was essential, as she never knew what time of day or night she would be called out how many miles she might have to trudge through the snow to get to whoever needed her special knowledge and skills.

Opening the reservoir on the side of the black Majestic range, she scooped out several dippers of hot water and poured them into the dishpan. Granny always claimed that a woman thought better with her hands immersed in hot water, whether washing dishes or clothing. It was true this time. Halfway through the dishes, Meghan raised her head, and a smile broke across her face. The canning could wait. What she had just thought of was as important as getting the garden harvested and into the glass jars, wasn't it?

She nodded her head, and a feeling of freedom ran

through her body. She grabbed a dishcloth and dried her hands, then spread the towel over the clean plates resting on the counter. They could wait too. She'd put them away later. Now, Meghan was going to give in and do what her heart had wanted to do ever since she had stood on the porch, reveling in the autumn colors and the crisp fall air.

She was going hiking. But it wasn't hiking just for the pure joy of being out in God's beauty. No, it was hiking with a purpose. She was going to make herself a sandwich, grab a tart apple, and put them in the canvas bag she had sewn especially for this type of errand. She had designed the bag to resemble a knapsack she could loop both arms through and carry the contents on her back, leaving her hands free to hold the stout walking stick that accompanied her on her forays into the woods, looking for herbs.

Today, she would go farther from the cabin than she usually hunted. Today she would hike toward the base of Yogo Gulch, a narrow cleft in the limestone that had been widened by blasting quite a few years ago. This area had several small mines owned by struggling miners looking for the elusive sapphires or gold. It also had a mountainside covered with wild roses. Wild roses that in the fall of the year sported fat orange berries called rose hips. Meghan knew that when crushed and boiled in teas, these rose hips were invaluable in fighting winter colds.

She hadn't been to the area for several months. It wasn't that far from the cabin if you cut over the back side of the gulch. And if the trail led through the fiery red oak brush and the other fall bushes, each one brilliant in its special color, and if the air was fresh and tangy, and if Meghan's feet were light as she indulged herself in this worthwhile errand, and if she forgot for today her chores and obligations, would that be so wrong? No, thought Meghan as she pulled the straps of the knapsack over her wool shirt. Not wrong at all.

Chapter Four

Meghan rested on a rise in the gulch. Off in the distance she could see the biggest mine site, comprised of several groups of unpainted, rough bunkhouses. The owner had a group from Butte, Montana, working for him, each making three dollars a day and earning every penny of it.

Years ago, when she was much younger, she had accompanied Granny to the big English-owned mine during an outbreak of influenza. The owner had come to Pig Eye Gulch to ask Granny to bring her herbs and expertise. She had willingly gone, taking Meghan along with her. After one day in the rough-and-tumble community, Granny said she needed to return to Pig Eye Gulch and her cabin for more herbs. When Granny returned to the mine the next morning, Meghan wasn't with her.

27

Granny came back with many stories about the Englishman. Whenever the owner traveled on business, he carried along several homing pigeons for communicating with the miners. Granny said that, while she was there, he sent a message out and got a return answer a few short hours later. He also used the pigeons to communicate with his men working the twelve-mile-long ditch-and-flume system. This system was vital to the mine, as it diverted water from Yogo Creek. The men kept cages of carrier pigeons as they inspected the ditch. A pigeon could carry a note in a leg capsule describing a problem; soon, an answer would come winging back to them. Granny had held one of the birds, and it had hunkered down, resting easy in her hands.

At the end of the outbreak, Granny was paid for her days of doctoring. As she was leaving, the owner handed her a roll of heavy muslin. She unrolled it to find two stones, each a brilliant blue and similar in size. The Englishman rubbed his thumb over them, telling Granny they were Yogo sapphires. Granny said the radiant color was called Montana blue. She had watched the miners separating the fool's gold from the sapphires in the sluices. The mine owner told her that her Montana blue Yogo sapphires were worthy to be displayed with others he had already sent to a prominent jeweler in Seattle, Washington. He offered to send hers there and, once sold, send the money her way. Granny thanked him but said the stones meant more to her than money. What she didn't tell him was the Montana blue Yogo radiated the same sparkle and intensity that she often saw in her precious

Meghan's eyes. Granny had shown the stones to Meghan, then rolled them back up safely in the muslin. *"These are yours, Meghan. Someday we'll have them made into a pair of earrings for you."*

"Someday" never came, but Meghan kept the blue stones safe in the muslin wrapper, hidden in a glass jar with the money and other blue stones she'd received from miners. But none were as beautiful, none as alive with shining facets, as her two Montana blues.

Meghan turned away from the distant town and continued her walk along a small creek as it twisted and twined through the brilliant bushes. Occasionally the water disappeared, swallowed up by undergrowth or a hole in the earth, only to emerge later, cold and clear from its underground journey. Meghan lost track of time as she followed the creek, picking the rose hips hanging fat on the branches of the bushes. Glancing up at the sky, she was surprised to see the sun so high and knew it was getting close to lunchtime. Her eyes confirmed her what her stomach already knew. She glanced down the creek and saw a copse of willows, their leaves forming a secluded enclosure, an invitation to her to enjoy her meal there.

Meghan was humming softly to herself when she first heard the sound. She stopped and listened. Nothing. Only the sound of the shallow creek rolling over copper-colored rocks. She shook her head and took a few steps, only to stop once more. Yes. There it was again. Meghan cocked her head in the direction of the sound. It came from the other side of the copse of willows. Slowly, quietly, she headed in that direction, unable to put a name to the sound yet sure it was a familiar one.

As Meghan came closer to the trees, the sound intensified, then came and went, fading into complete stillness. Meghan stopped suddenly. She knew the sound. Yet it couldn't be. She listened with every fiber of her being. Nothing. Complete silence. She started forward again, and this time when it came, there was no denying it: the cry of a baby, angry and loud in the whispering stillness of the trees. Without thinking, Meghan ran crashing through the trees, her knapsack and hair catching in the branches and bushes as she pushed her way through. She came to an abrupt stop in a clearing, her breath catching in her throat as she stared at a cabin. The cries were angrier now, louder and unceasing. Slowly Meghan moved to the porch, her moccasin-clad feet making no sound. She tried to peer in the one small window, but it hadn't been washed since several rains, and the dust blocked out what little view there might have been.

Meghan cleared her throat. The cries broke off into long, shuddering sobs. Something was wrong. The thought gave her the strength to call out. "Hello. Is anybody home?" Her words hung in the air. "Hello!" she called louder and more forcefully. Silence followed. Then the crying started up again. But the tone of the cry had changed from anger to questioning hopefulness. Meghan took a deep breath and put her hand on the door handle, her thumb lightly on the latch. Resolutely she pressed downward and was surprised as the door swung open. Meghan stepped inside, gently shutting the door behind her. She stood there, letting her eyes get used to the darkness of the room. A foul odor reached her nostrils and, together with the loud cries, brought a sense of despair to the scene.

Standing in a pen, for it could be called nothing else, a baby girl sobbed as if her heart would break. The pen was made up of strips of canvas wrapped around various pieces of furniture, forming a rough circle of three or four feet diameter. In the center of the circle, standing on wobbly legs, was a bonneted little girl. Meghan moved closer. The baby never took her eyes off her but emitted a low, sobbing hiccup every few seconds. Her long, once white gown clung to her damp bottom, and her thick-stockinged legs buckled and swayed as she held on to the rail of a chair. The face peering out from the bonnet was smudged, and tears ran from her big blue eyes down cheeks chapped and rosy. Teardrops glistened on long eyelashes. Giving one loud hiccup, the baby sat down hard on her bottom and stuck two grimy fingers into her small mouth. She blinked a couple of times, then, around the sides of the two chubby fingers, came a small, hesitant smile.

Meghan leaned over the makeshift pen and, without thinking, lifted the smelly child into her arms. "My," she whispered, "you're a miserable little doll, aren't you?"

The baby took the two wet fingers out of her mouth and touched them to Meghan's cheek. The eyes studying her were solemn and unblinking.

"You need some attention, honey," Meghan whispered

to the little girl. "Where's your mommy, huh?" Meghan looked around the open room. It wasn't clean, but it wasn't dirty, either. It was—and the word popped into Meghan's mind—*disheveled,* as if the woman keeping house didn't know what she was doing. Or perhaps just didn't care, thought Meghan as she wrinkled her nose at the pen in the center of the floor.

Meghan started to move away from the pen with the baby, when she was stopped short by a long strip of sheet tied around the baby's middle, stretching back to the leg of a heavy chair, where it was securely tied. "Someone wanted to make darn sure you didn't get away," she muttered to the bonneted head now nestled on her shoulder. Meghan walked back to the pen, but when she tried to set the baby back inside the enclosure so she could untie the sheet holding her there, the child stiffened and gave another loud cry.

"Hush, sweetie, I'm only going to leave you there a second. I have to untie you. See?" Meghan's fingers quickly began untying the knot, but the baby only understood she'd been rescued, then returned to the dismal pen. Meghan worked with the knot as her eyes surveyed the contents of the pen. She grudgingly admitted that someone had taken every precaution to keep the baby safe and as contented and comfortable as possible during her confinement. Thick pads of blankets covered the wooden floor. Small pillows were scattered about, making it easy for a little head to lie on them. Two bottles, one empty, one half full of milk, lay to one side. There was a piece of hard toast in a corner, and beside one quilt lay a hand-sewn cloth doll with yarn for hair alongside a small wooden horse. The blankets, pillowcases, and the child's gown looked as if they had been washed in the creek and were a dingy gray, but they weren't dirty as she'd first thought. Neither was the child, Meghan thought as she picked her up, freeing her from the loosened strip of sheet. No, she wasn't dirty, just badly in need of a change. Meghan carried her to a double bed in a corner of the room. It looked as if it had been hastily made, and the plaid wool blanket covering it was crooked, hanging longer in the front than in the back.

"Where are your diapers, baby girl?" Meghan said to the big-eyed doll watching her as she lay still on the bed. Glancing around the room, Meghan saw a pile of diapers on the top shelf of a homemade dresser. They were as gray as the rest of the baby's clothing, but they were clean and dry.

Meghan brought one back to the bed and began to change the smelly diaper. "Whew!" she said. "I'd cry too if I had to wear this. You poor thing." Meghan wiped the child as clean as possible, then went to the enamel basin resting on a table. Keeping the child in sight, she poured a dipper of water over one diaper, wetting it, and went back to the baby lying there watching her every movement. "There now, honey, that has to feel better, doesn't it?"

"Come here." She picked up the little girl. "Your nightie's damp, but at least it isn't against your skin. Where on earth is your mother? Huh?" She whispered the questions softly as she patted the baby's back. "Someone loves you, little girl. Enough to look out for you while they were gone. The child snuggled against her chest, spent from her bout of crying.

"Are you hungry, little one?" Meghan went back to the pen for the half-full bottle of milk. The child stiffened in her arms. "Don't worry, I'm not putting you back in . . . at least not for a while. Surely your mother will be returning any time now." Meghan popped the nipple off the bottle and smelled the milk. Fresh. She put the nipple back on and sat down in one of the chairs, the baby cuddled in the crook of her arm. She put the nipple into the little girl's rosebud mouth, and with blue eyes staring at her, softly began to hum. After a few minutes of watching her, the baby started sucking on the nipple.

Meghan watched the child as she pulled on the nipple, her eyes growing heavy, closing, then popping open, only to close again, each time longer and longer until they remained shut, the long lashes fanned out against the roughened cheeks.

"You are so beautiful." Meghan marveled at the perfectly formed child, her tiny nose, her long lashes, and her blond curls sticking out from the sides of her bonnet. Tiny hands with short nails gripped the bottle. Meghan raised her head, looking away from the sleeping baby to the cluttered cabin. She was trespassing in a woman's home, holding her baby. A sense of urgency filled her, and she slowly rose to her feet. She didn't want to be there when the baby's mother returned. She sensed that she would be unwelcome, an intruder. Meghan walked to the pen and lay the sleeping baby on one of the pillows. Covering her with a quilt, Meghan leaned over and kissed her softly on one cherub cheek.

"I'll be back," she whispered in the still of the cabin. Whoever leaves you alone here must love you, but, darn her, this is no way to treat a baby. No way at all, and I'm going to tell her that. In no uncertain terms."

She picked up her knapsack and the soiled diaper and left the cabin, gently shutting the door behind her. She walked to the creek and rinsed out the diaper and hung it on a bush. She pulled the knapsack across her back in preparation for her walk back to her own cabin. But she couldn't leave. She took the knapsack off and dropped it to her feet. It was no use. Intruder or not, she couldn't walk off and leave that baby girl alone.

"I won't be watching over you from inside the cabin, but I'll watch over you nonetheless." She sat down in the deep grass, a boulder for a backrest, and settled in to keep vigil. She could see the cabin, but unless someone knew just where to look, she was hidden from sight. Several times during the wait she left her spot to go peek in the window at the still-sleeping child, reassuring herself all was okay.

The day slowly faded into dusk before Meghan saw a shadowy figure open the door to the cabin and step inside. Not wanting to risk being seen, she crept forward and listened at the door. Hearing a delighted squeal of welcome from the baby and a soft, crooning response, she knew the baby's parent was home. She could leave now. Quietly, she started in the direction of her own home. Giving one last glance at the cabin that was gradually being swallowed up by the tall willows surrounding it, Meghan again felt the velvet baby cheek. A cheek that had held for a brief moment the softness of Meghan's kiss.

Chapter Five

Meghan rolled over in her bed. Thunder crashed across the Big Snowy Mountains with such a force, the whole cabin shook. She pulled the quilt tighter around her, trying to block out the sound. Again it came, and again, but this time it was accompanied by a man's voice.

"Miss Meghan! Miss Meghan!" Each word was punctuated by the thunder that shook the cabin door.

Meghan rose sleepily up on one arm. Then her heart jumped into her throat. It wasn't thunder shaking her front door. It was someone's fist.

"Miss Meghan, you got to come quick!"

Meghan jumped out of bed, fully awake, and grabbed Granny's quilted robe. Throwing it on, she made her way through the semidarkness. Each step she took was accompanied by the calling of her name and a fist to the door. Her mind raced with the possibilities of the urgency being beaten on the door. It was too early for Tilly Stoddard's baby. If it was the baby, she'd lose it for sure. Meghan recalled the woman's last birthing and the long, difficult labor. Her thoughts flew, as did her feet.

She jerked open the door to be met by a man's fist, raised for yet another pummeling attack on her door.

"Good gosh Almighty, miss, you got to come with me. Now." A young man stood there in a state of semidress. His pants had been pulled on over a red union suit, a suspender over one shoulder, the other looped and hanging. He wore no shirt or coat to ward off the chill morning air.

Meghan didn't recognize him, but there were always new miners and prospectors coming and going through the Judith Valley.

She clutched the front of the robe tighter. "Please, slow down. I have no idea what you want or need, and I have no intention of going anywhere with you until I do. Now, what's the emergency?" She moved to the side of the partially opened door and rested her hand on the shotgun propped out of sight against the wall.

"It's . . . it's . . ." The man took a deep breath to steady himself. "Our baby's been burned, miss." The words came tumbling out, coated with fear and urgency. "We was up early—I got the first shift—and my wife was frying some salt pork. She turned her back. Only for a second, miss," he said, imploring her to understand. "The baby, he's walking and into everything. He's real fast." Meghan could hear pride mixed with fear in the young father's voice, but her mind was already racing to what she would need to bring along. "I don't know how he reached"—he gulped—"he reached the handle of the frying pan and pulled . . . The grease . . ."

"It's okay." Meghan stopped the words. She knew all she needed to know. "I have to get dressed and pack supplies. I won't be but a minute. You wait here on the porch and try to get your breath." Meghan closed the door.

Comfrey, red clover blossoms, nettles, skullcap, marshmallow. The names flew through her mind like a litany. Meghan rushed around the kitchen, packing the herbs in her knapsack. "I need the aloe vera gel. That I'll put on immediately. Now, for pain, I'll take echinacea, maybe some kava kava powder. Yes, that might be best. I won't know until I see the baby . . . how badly he's burned." She wasn't aware she was speaking the words aloud. All she knew was that in emergencies like this, while she was pulling on clothes and trying to think what she might need, imagining every possibility, time seemed to stand still. She would have to go into the root cellar for the kava kava and a few of the other herbs she wanted.

The more commonly used ones Meghan kept in a chest in the kitchen. The others, the ones that didn't grow around here, Granny had gotten from a mail-order pharmacy in Seattle. These were kept in the root cellar. They cost money, and great care was taken to see that not a leaf or stem was wasted. Many a night Granny had sat at the table reading the flyers describing the different herbs and their medicinal value, the kerosene lantern sputtering and sending shadows into the room. *"Listen here, kid,"* she'd say as Meghan lay in her bed, half asleep, *"this here one's named"*—and her tongue would curl around the strange-sounding name, giving it her own pronunciation. *"Well, can you believe it can do that?"* She'd lick the tip of her pencil and add that name to her order.

Meghan thrust her arms into her heavy wool coat, grabbed the knapsack, and went out the door. She quickly told the waiting man to stay where he was; she'd be right back. She held the kerosene lantern in front of her, picking off the shelves the needed herbs. Once back outside, she turned the lantern valve to off, letting the lingering glow from the two gaskets light the waiting man's face.

"It's getting light. I think we can see without a lantern."

The man tersely nodded, then turned and struck out ahead of Meghan.

There was no talking as they crashed through the brush and trees. Several times Meghan didn't catch a branch quickly enough, and it snapped back and caught her in the face or arm. There was no apology from the man ahead of her. His thoughts, like hers, were on the child waiting for them.

The cabin hovered on the edge of town. The man threw open the door to a strangely silent room. "Marybeth, I'm back, and I've got that doctorin' lady."

Meghan followed him into the one-room shack. Her first impression was of neatness, then of poverty. Meghan had seen all too many of these cabins and shacks. They seemed to spring up with a life of their own around the mines. People came full of hope and dreams, and after a time most left, their dreams gone along with their youth. The mine was a demanding mistress, taking lifeblood and giving back little in return. Some made it on their own by finding enough gold or sapphires to make it worth the backbreaking work. The smart ones took their find and ran. But most stayed looking, hoping for the bigger stone, the better vein.

Meghan crossed the room to where a pale woman sat holding a quietly sobbing little boy. The mother's eyes were wide with fright as she tried to cope with an everyday morning turned into a nightmare. The child, curled up on her lap, sobbed mournfully, shuddering. He was nearly spent with crying, reduced to the racking moans of pain. Meghan lightly touched the mother's shoulder. She was young. Younger than Meghan.

"We thank you for coming, ma'am." Tears pooled in the woman's eyes. "We done everything we knew to do, but we don't have any medicine, and he's . . . he's in bad pain."

Meghan hoped that what they had done so far wasn't something that would worsen an already bad situation.

"I'm glad to come. I'll do my best, I promise. Now, what's his name?" Meghan smiled at the infant, his face hidden, pressed into his mother's breast.

"Jimmy," both parents whispered, love etched in the one word.

"I need to look at him. Will he let me?"

The mother nodded and pulled the child away from her. "Jimmy, my love, this nice lady's here to help us. She's going to make it all better."

Meghan drew in her breath as she saw the angry red stain of burned skin starting at the baby's throat, then splotching his small chest. Then she saw his arm. It had taken the brunt of the hot grease. The child held it pitifully out to her, his eyes wary and glazed.

"Ow," he sobbed.

"I know it hurts, love. I know it does," Meghan crooned to him.

She straightened up from the child. His neck and chest had been somewhat protected by his clothing, but the small bare arm had been completely exposed. Thank God his face hadn't been burned, because Meghan knew that the arm would scar.

The moment she entered the cabin, Meghan had become the healer, the person the town looked to as the one who could help. The one with the knowledge and answers. All thoughts left her mind but that of the child needing her ministrations. Three sets of eyes looked to her. Three people felt her strength and took heart in it.

"Sit him up on the table. It will be easier for me to do what I must if he's sitting upright."

The mother rose with the baby, faltered, and was steadied by the man. It was then that Meghan realized that the woman was expecting. A sadness washed over Meghan. Two babies, and she was so young and . . . and poor. She took a deep breath. Her only concern now, her only reason for being here, was the small boy held by his mother.

The father hurried to the table and removed the few dishes there. He put a quilt down, the star pattern clean and bright, and helped the mother place the baby on the quilt.

"It's okay, my little man. It's okay." He whispered the words to the child, a look of love and pride on his face. "You be tough for your dad, okay? I'll be standing' right here."

The little boy nodded his head through the pain and fear. His eyes were wide as they watched Meghan's every movement.

Meghan laid her herbs, a small wooden bowl, spoons, a wooden pestle, her jars, and clean cloths out at the child's side.

"I need hot water to wash my hands, please," she told the father. She didn't look up as she readied her equipment. She knew that the task ahead would not be easy. Her kind of work never was. Seeing people suffering always left its mark on her, but nothing hurt as much as a child in pain. Still, Meghan knew that, through it all, she had the power to help ease that pain and to heal.

"Now," she said to the mother, "tell me what you have done so far."

"I . . . I put his arm in a bucket of cold water." The mother's voice was hesitant, laced with fear that she had done something wrong. I put a cold rag over his chest. I didn't know what else to do," she moaned. "I just wanted to stop the burning."

"You did right," Meghan said, giving her confirmation she badly needed. "If these burns were kept in cold water long enough, he won't be getting any blisters."

"I kept the cold water on them right up to my sitting

down to hold him, just a few minutes before you walked in the door," the mother said hopefully.

"Good," Meghan answered her, examining the small chest and arm in front of her. "Mr. . . . uh . . ." She glanced up at the man. "I'm sorry, I don't know your name."

"Phillips. Emery Phillips, and this here's my wife, Marybeth. You already met Jimmy."

He introduced his small family.

"Mr. Phillips . . ."

"Emery. Mr. Phillips is my dad."

"Fine." Meghan smiled, "Emery, would you see that the stove is kept well stocked with wood? Jimmy has had quite a shock, and we don't want him chilled." She looked at the little boy sitting in the center of the wooden table, tears trickling down his cheeks, sobs wracking his body as he tried to be tough.

"Now, Jimmy, I'm going to have to take a real good look at those burns, because I have to make sure they are clean.

Meghan walked to a basin filled with hot water. She picked up the bar of homemade soap resting there and scrubbed her hands. Then she walked back to the family, their eyes following her every movement. Gently she touched the small boy's chest, peering closely at the redness. He moved away from her touch and gave a low cry.

"Jimmy." His dad spoke the one word, and immediately the child held himself still for Meghan's examination.

Thank God, Meghan thought. *It's as I first suspected. His shirt saved him.* While the skin was red, Meghan knew it was scalded, unlike the deep, blistering injury on his arm. Still, scalded or burned, the pain was intense.

The child's arm would have to wait. There was a more serious problem hovering: shock. She'd seen grown men go into shock after a bad injury, and Jimmy was a child, with a child's delicate system.

"Marybeth," Meghan said as she handed her a small pouch. "Make this into a tea. Then, when the powder is absorbed by the hot water, add this." She handed her a smaller pouch. "It's a special tea," she said in answer to the questioning look. "It must be hot to blend, but after the blending, you can add some cold water. Not much. Only enough to cool it so Jimmy will drink it." She turned away from the mother. "Jimmy, your mother is making you a fine-tasting tea. You must drink every drop. Can I depend on you to do that?"

"You can, miss. My boy will do whatever he must." The father laid a calloused hand on the small boy's yellow hair.

"Thank you, Emery. It's vital that Jimmy not go into shock. This tea will help us fight that. It's what we call a stimulant. The pouches I gave Marybeth were ginger and lavender, crushed and ready for the hot water. We can expect Jimmy to become very tired quite soon. He's had a terrible shock to his little system, and that will be his way of coping. First I treat the shock, then we must do something for the pain." Without realizing it, Meghan was parroting her Granny's off-spoken words. Words of comfort and explanation she had absorbed as though through her very skin while standing by the wise woman's side, watching and learning from every sickness or accident Granny had attended to. She had started out as helpless as a child whose only duty was not to get in the way. Then, as she grew up, she became a helpmate.

Marybeth came to Meghan's side and held out the cup of tea. Meghan smiled. "You give it to him. I'm a stranger. He'll take it better from you." Meghan stepped aside and watched as the little boy took a hesitant sip of the tea. A bigger sip followed as he found the mixture pleasant in both smell and taste. He took several more sips of the brew, then stopped and shook his head.

The young father placed his hand back on the child's head. "All of it, my man. Every last drop."

The words were spoken softly, but they worked like magic. The little boy opened his eyes even wider, then took two big gulps of the tea, finishing it off. The pain the child was experiencing had to be severe, yet his desire to please his father and to earn the pride that flared from the man's eyes overrode his agony. Meghan had never wanted so badly to take a small face into her hands and plant a gentle kiss on the wide forehead partially covered by an unruly shock of hair the color of the gold his dad labored for.

Now she would ease his pain. "Some water, please, Emery. But this time it must be lukewarm. Oh, and be sure the basin has been scalded clean."

She opened her knapsack and pulled out yet another

small bottle. "Jimmy, this is called witch hazel. It has a lovely smell, see?" And she held the small vial under his nose. The smell was good, and she hoped it would have the effect on the child she wanted, that of easing his fear of the unknown. "Now, I'm going to pour the witch hazel into the pan of water your father just brought me. Then do you know what I'll do next? Of course you don't. I'm going to bathe everywhere you've been burned. And, Jimmy, one thing you can count on, I will always tell you the truth."

She paused to be sure she had his full attention. "This will hurt. It will hurt some here"—she pointed to his small chest—"but it will hurt very badly here"—and she pointed to his arm, red with angry marks running from his round little shoulder to just above a chubby wrist. As Meghan pointed to his arm, she saw what she had hoped not to see. Blisters. There was one large one covering the inside of the child's arm and several smaller ones on the outer surface. The burns had been deep. Not only were these the most serious and difficult to heal, but they would leave permanent scars. Again Meghan gave thanks that the hot grease had missed the child's sweet face. She knew then that the mother's cold water hadn't been enough to draw the fire from the underside of the arm.

Talking softly to the child, she began washing the burns with the witch hazel solution. Even the softest touch brought cries and tears of pain from the stalwart little boy. Meghan raised her head once from the onerous task and saw that the tears on the child's face were joined by tears rolling unabashed from the father's eyes.

And perhaps worse than the pain was the parents' desperate feeling of helplessness. Their precious child was now in the care of a stranger.

Meghan paused in her task, seeing the child sway, barely able to sit upright on the table. Exhaustion, pain, and shock were setting in. Meghan felt a sense of urgency. She had to finish her task quickly. Her nimble fingers flew as she grabbed her bowl and began mixing a paste of herbs. "Emery, drape a quilt over his shoulders. He must be kept warm. Marybeth, you talk to him. I don't want him asleep until we've finished bandaging the burns and he drinks more tea or some broth. Do you have anything we can make a broth of, perhaps some . . . ?" She stopped, seeing the flush on the woman's face and the embarrassed drop of the father's eyes.

"No," she said quickly, answering her own question, looking away from the parents. "No, it has to be a special broth. A . . . a medicine broth. Yes, a medicine broth, and I'm sorry, Marybeth, but you couldn't possibly have the ingredients. But I do back at my cabin. I'll finish the bandaging and return to my cabin for the broth. We'll make do with the tea Jimmy had earlier. This time we'll add some of the honey I'm mixing into this paste."

She smiled at the parents as they watched her pour the thick brown honey into the bowl. "This will keep the burn from getting infected," she explained. The rest of the herbs are comfrey root that I've ground into powder, lobelia, and wheat germ. Mixed with the honey, like this"—she showed them the thickened paste—"it will easily cover each burn. I'll smear some aloe vera on the smaller burns. It will be cool and soothing. Now," she said, as she began wrapping bandages around the small arm and chest, "these must not be disturbed for three days. This will allow time for new skin to grow and cover where the other was burned off." She finished the last bandage on the drowsy child, now held upright by his father. A pleased look crossed Meghan's face. The child had stopped crying. The comfrey paste and aloe vera gel were working.

"Marybeth, let's have some more hot water for Jimmy's tea. And, here"—she handed the jar of honey to the woman—"put plenty of this in the tea, and let's add some red clover blossoms. That, along with the echinacea, will help fight the pain from the inside as well as the outside." She spoke more to herself than to the young woman, who was busy preparing the drink.

The tea was brewed, and again Jimmy was coaxed to drink the entire cupful. He ran his small, pink tongue over his lips, licking the honey from them.

"I'll bet it would feel good to Jimmy just to be held and rocked," Meghan said to the mother. *Not only would it be good for Jimmy, it would be good for you too,* she thought. *You look as if you are about to drop.*

The dad caught Meghan's eye and nodded, then gently, as though the child would break, he wrapped him in the quilt and lifted the precious bundle from the table, following Marybeth to the handmade rocker and placing the child in her lap. Jimmy immediately lay his head against his mother's breast and gave in to a deep sleep.

Meghan backed away and motioned for Emery to follow her to a corner of the room. "I don't want to frighten you, Emery, but the next few days are risky. I'm afraid of fever. I'll do everything I can to prevent this from happening. Jimmy must be kept quiet, clean, warm, and"—she paused—"nourished. His body needs every tool to help him heal."

A red flush crept up the man's face and mixed with the fatigue etched around his eyes. Here was a man who rarely saw the light of day, as he gave most of his waking moments to a mine that, in return, gave him three dollars a day.

"Uh, Miss Meghan, I guess you can see, we ain't got much. I started here to work a week ago, and I got another week to go before I get any money. Me'n 'Marybeth been gettin' by on what little we brought from Colorado. We give the most to Jimmy. Don't get me wrong"—he gave her a quick look—"we ain't mindin' that. He's the most important. But still, 'the most' ain't very much." He ducked his head. "I'll go to the store and see if I can beg some credit. The owner don't like to give credit to miners he don't know. Can't say as I blame him." He lowered his voice. "Us new ones are usually the first to get in the way of an accident. We ain't mine-smart yet. He be losin' money on us. But maybe if I tell him . . ." He stopped talking and reached for his coat hanging on a peg by the door. His movement was determined, and Meghan knew that he'd do his best to get credit for the food his boy needed. But Meghan also knew that the store owner, Mr. Roberts, was as hard as nails.

Pig Eye Gulch was a mining town, filled with men who came and went before you hardly knew they were around. Life was expendable here. Roberts' General Store had been around since Pig Eye Gulch had sprung up around the earliest mines; Meghan had no doubt it would be there when others had closed. She didn't hold out much hope for Emery's chances of credit.

"Emery," she said to the man. "Just a minute. Now that I helped you, would you be willing to help me?"

He turned slowly back, a puzzled look on his face. "Course I would. I'd do most anything for you, Miss Meghan. I owe you more than I'll ever be able to pay. Just to see my boy resting comfortably in his mother's arms is worth my life to me. I'd give you anything I had. But the fact is, I don't have a darn thing."

"Of course you do," Meghan said forcefully. "You have a strong back, don't you?"

A rueful smile flickered across the man's lips. "That I do. I'm strong."

"Then you are just what I need." Meghan rushed ahead. "I have been trying to clean out my root cellar to get ready for this year's canning and storing. I raised a bigger garden this year and don't believe I'll have enough room on the shelves for all I plan to put up." She paused, searching for words that would convince a proud man to accept a gift. "I need to clear out jars that have been on the shelves a couple of years. The food's still good, but I can't eat it up in time. Bad as I hate to, I'm going to have to haul it to a ravine and dump it. It's a shame, but I need the space. Better I get rid of the old than let the new rot in the ground. You're not going to be able to work today—not now, are you?"

"No," Emery said hesitantly. "It's past my shift time, and the sinking bucket's already gone down."

"Well, they say it's an ill wind that blows no one some good. I need someone to haul the excess out of my cellar. Just haul it out and dump it in the ravine. I'll pay you for your time. Shame, but I don't know what else to do. Say," she said, "would you be wanting any of the stores? No, I suppose not. They're a year or two old. Still, it would be a sight better use of it, Emery, than spilling it down a mountainside."

She waited expectantly.

"Stores?"

"Yes, there's some apples and potatoes left. Onions, turnips, carrots—oh, and, of course, jars of vegetables, canned meat, preserves." She said the words with studied indifference.

"You mean you intend to throw that food away?"

"If I must. I have to make room for this year's storage."

"Spoiled?"

"What?"

"Is it spoiled?"

"Heavens, no, its not spoiled. I opened a jar of the apple butter last night. Had it on my bread. It was delicious. I just don't have room, and can't think what else . . ."

The man cleared his throat. "We'd . . . I'd be real pleased to take what you plan to throw out, Miss Meghan. I won't take no money from you, no way. But the food would . . . I won't take anything you weren't planning on getting rid of, though," he said proudly.

"Of course not. I need my preserving and stores myself. But"—she paused, as if giving his offer some thought—"well, I agree. It's a deal. You take the excess storage, and I'll get my cellar cleaned. Sounds like a fair deal." She held out her hand to the man.

He took her hand in his calloused one and shook it. He looked away. "A fair deal," he muttered under his breath as he turned once again toward the door. "More than a fair deal—a godsend."

Meghan put her wool coat back on and followed Emery Phillips out the door. She felt a burst of lightness, and she turned and gave one last look at the mother and child sitting in the chair, both sets of eyes closed as sleep claimed them. The child rested peacefully in his mother's arms.

Meghan's thoughts flashed to another child, a child she had forced herself not to think about as she put all her thoughts and energy into coping with the day's emergency. Blond curls and a small rosebud mouth. A child, left alone in a makeshift pen in a lonely cabin.

She had promised Rose—for that was the name she had given the child—that she would return. Rose, because if she hadn't been picking the fruit of the wild roses, she wouldn't have heard her cries. She wouldn't have held in her arms the precious little girl.

A majority of the day would be devoted to Jimmy and his family. She helped Emery get his first load of stores, then, explaining to him that she had another patient she had to check on, left him to his task and without a backward glance hurried along the path that would lead to the cabin and Rose.

At her first sight of the cabin, she took a deep breath and boldly walked up to the door and gave a sharp rap. There was no response. No sound came from within. Reluctant to knock again and possibly wake a sleeping baby, Meghan peeked in the window. The cabin was empty. Her first feeling was that of disappointment, followed by relief that there was no baby alone occupying a pen. "I'm still going to have a talk with your mother, Rose," she said as she turned and started tracing her way back to her home. *Tomorrow. I'll be back tomorrow. No matter what. I have to see how my Rose is faring. No matter what.*

Chapter Six

It was midafternoon before Meghan was able to grab a light jacket and set off across the gulch for the cabin and Rose. She had spent the morning with Jimmy and Marybeth Phillips. Emery had worked until the last light of day hauling foodstuff from Meghan's root cellar to his home. Each trip, he seemed to stand a little taller as he provided for his family. Meghan thanked God for that overstocked cellar.

She had awakened early and left immediately for the Phillipes'. She had no worry that she'd arrive before they were awake. She knew that the first shift at the mine started long before sunup. She also knew that Emery would be there, ready to start his twelve-hour shift. His family couldn't afford his missing another day's pay.

She carried with her some staples from her own

kitchen. Marybeth would not be as difficult to convince to accept them. "Consider them a loan," Meghan told her.

Marybeth smiled at Meghan's words, and in that smile of understanding shared between two women, a friendship was born. Meghan had never had a friend, and Marybeth desperately needed one.

Meghan was pleased to see Jimmy sitting on a stool at the table, eating a bowl of applesauce. The child looked up at her and smiled through the sticky sauce smeared from nose to chin. "Ghan," he said when he saw her, then went back to scooping the remains of the applesauce from the bowl.

"That's the best I can get him to do with your name," apologized Marybeth.

Meghan ran her hands across the child's head, then sat down across from him. "He seems to be doing okay for himself," she chuckled, as a spoonful of applesauce missed the open mouth and deposited most of the fruit on the small chin.

"He only woke up once during the night. I did as you said. I gave him some more of that tea. He went right back to sleep and slept until his dad got up. He always gets up with his dad to see him off. Sat right there on that stool, sassy as ever. I don't know what's in that tea, Miss Meghan, but it's a miracle drink, that it is."

"Meghan."

"What?"

"No *miss*. Just Meghan. Friends don't call each other

miss, and I've no doubt that you and I are going to be friends, Marybeth."

Marybeth nodded her agreement, a smile of delight on her round face. "Yes," she said, "I'm sure we will be. And"—she rubbed her swollen stomach—"I've no doubt I'll be needing my *friend's* help again in a few months."

"I'll be here," Meghan promised. She turned back to Jimmy. "His bandage still in place?"

"Yes. I was careful not to disturb it this morning when I dressed him. His chest don't seem to pain him much. It's his arm."

"Yes, that's the worst of the burns. I have hope that the paste I put on will draw the fire, and when we take the bandage off in another day or so, we'll see the blisters flattened." Meghan didn't say aloud that her greatest fear was taking the bandage off and finding increased redness and drainage from the blisters, telling her the burn was infected. She shook her head. She wouldn't think that way. She'd seen Granny use this paste and had seen the results. If it worked for Granny, surely it would work for her.

Meghan smiled as Marybeth put a cup of tea in front of her.

"It's some you sent. I made Emery a cup this morning. He liked it fine, but he said it didn't compare none to coffee. I'll bet coffee's the first thing he'll buy this Saturday when he gets his pay."

"I should have thought of coffee," Meghan said. "I have to have it myself on awakening. How stupid of me."

" 'Stupid'? When you gave us all this?" She waved at the wooden crates nailed to the wall next to the kitchen range, now serving as shelves filled with jars from Meghan's root cellar. Sitting under the rough cupboards were gunnysacks of apples, potatoes, onions, and other vegetables. "You saved us from some very lean days, Meghan. And, bless you, you saved Emery's pride." Marybeth's look told her new friend that she knew the "cleaning" of the root cellar had been a sham. It told Meghan she knew but understood and accepted the kindness in the spirit it was given.

Meghan stayed only long enough to assure herself that Jimmy was doing well and, with the resilience of youth, seemed to be bouncing back from his ordeal. His only concession to the burns was when some movement would jar the arm he carefully guarded. Then he would cry out, "Ow! Ow!"

The first time he did this, he turned to his mother, who turned to Meghan.

Meghan took two pouches from her sack. She opened the small canvas bags and scooped out a spoonful each of the pulverized herbs. She put them into a cup and stirred in a few drops of water, making a paste of the mixture. "This is something to help the pain. It's camomile and catnip along with a couple of other herbs. Give him a spoonful of this every few hours. In between, use the tea. It's full of pain relievers and blood purifiers to help with the healing. But most of all, Marybeth, keep him clean and dry. The bandaging must be kept intact."

Jimmy opened his mouth like a little bird when

Meghan dipped the tip of the spoon filled with the thick paste into some of his applesauce and offered it to him. Both she and Marybeth chuckled at his face when he discovered the spoon held something more than the delicious sauce.

Then, after that, whenever he'd move the injured arm wrong, he cry out his "Ow" and add "Ghan" to the litany.

Meghan felt her heart fill the first time he did this and went immediately to the child, and, taking his messy face in her hands, kissed his upturned nose. "You are a heartbreaker, Jimmy Phillips. Not only sweet, you even taste good." And she licked a drop of applesauce from her lips.

She felt guilty leaving so soon. Marybeth was clearly disappointed. She had plainly planned on having her new friend spend a few hours to help ease her loneliness in the small isolated shack as she waited for the evening whistle to blow, signaling another shift and Emery's return.

Meghan would have liked nothing better. But now that she'd fulfilled her obligation to her small patient, she wanted to be off in another direction. Off through the brush, to follow the creek that led to Yogo Gulch.

Again Meghan heard no cries. In fact, the stillness was so deep, she found herself approaching the cabin with trepidation. She paused in the clearing out front and waited, listening. Nothing. She crossed the clearing and lightly placed one moccasined foot on the first step. Still nothing. It was as if the cabin was abandoned, devoid of human life for a long time. But Meghan knew better. And once more she had the mixed feeling of relief and disappointment. Relief that the baby girl had not been left alone again, tied inside a rude pen. Disappointment because she'd looked forward to seeing Rose again. The child had touched Meghan in a surprising way.

She wrinkled her brow, then shrugged her shoulders. *As long as I'm here, I might as well make myself known. I'm sure no one's about, but, well, I've come this far— might as well knock.* She swiftly crossed the porch and, before she would allow herself to think about it, gave a strong knock on the solid door. No answer.

Just as I thought. She turned away from the door and started back down the steps. Then she stopped. *It wouldn't hurt to look in the window. Make absolutely sure. After all, it's not as if I'm . . . Oh, stop, Meghan,* she chided herself. *Look in the window. It's not the first time, and you know you want to.*

Resolutely she crossed to the window and peered inside. Her breath caught in her throat. The pen was still there. And there in the middle of the pen lay the baby. Rose. She was on her stomach with her knees drawn up under her, her small rump in the air. Today there was no bonnet, and her blond curls lay tight against her head. She was wearing another dingy gray-white nightgown, and on her legs were the same thick stockings.

Meghan pulled away from the window and went back to the door. Again the latch responded to her pressure, and the door opened. Meghan shut it softly behind her and stood inside the room. It was empty save for the small body asleep in the pen. She went over to stand beside it, looking down at the tiny form sleeping in such an uncomfortable-looking position that Meghan gave a small chuckle.

She stood there for several minutes watching the sleeping child, then glanced around the large room. It was as neat as the other day. Neat in a haphazard manner, and again Meghan was filled with the sense that the woman keeping the house was new to what she was doing. The house lacked the touch most homemakers would unconsciously give it. On the counter, the dishpan was face up instead of being turned upside down to drain. The cracker tin had its lid off, leaving the crackers exposed to the air and whatever else might come along. The top of the range had a fine powder of dust. And over the back of every chair in the cabin was draped some article of baby clothing. Diapers, gowns, stockings, blankets, all draped as if to dry and all the same dingy gray. Still, in spite of the disarray, the cabin was pleasant and filled with the afternoon sunshine, homey and welcoming.

Meghan had an urge to tidy things up. It would only take a few minutes to have it in shape. She smiled at her fussiness. *Everything in its place, Meghan.* Well, nothing seemed to be in its place in this home, but, then, it wasn't her concern. She was only here, an uninvited guest, because of the precious baby starting to squirm herself awake on the heavy quilt. As Meghan watched, a tender smile on her face, the baby stretched out her legs, flattening her tummy against the quilt. She gave a few little squeaks and rolled over onto her back. Her eyes flew open, looking fully at Meghan, and at the same time two tiny fingers plopped into her small mouth.

"Hi, precious," Meghan whispered, afraid the child would be frightened to see someone standing there. "Do you remember me? Hmm? Don't be afraid, little Rose. I won't hurt you."

Meghan didn't move as she waited to see the child's response. She needn't have worried. The baby gave a delighted cry, rolled over to her knees, and pulled herself up to the side of the pen. Meghan moved toward her, while, at the same time, the baby worked herself closer by hanging on and taking small, unsteady steps. Meghan bent over and scooped up the little girl.

"Oh, honey, you're not a bit afraid, are you? Do you remember me? I remember you. In fact, I haven't been able to think of much else *but* you."

At these words, the baby pushed back against Meghan's chest and looked into her face, her blue eyes wide and questioning.

Meghan sucked in her breath. The child was beautiful. Her eyes were a deep blue with long blond lashes. Everything about her was delicate and perfect, from the top of her curly hair to the tips of her stocking-clad toes. It was as if someone had crafted a live, porcelain doll. Her nose was tiny, her chin was tiny, her ears were tiny, and her two fingers, again resting in her mouth, were tiny. Meghan snuggled her face against the warm spot under the baby's chin. "Mmm, you even smell sweet. Much better than last time." Meghan chuckled at the memory and inhaled the baby smell.

Holding the child, she untied the strip of sheet that held her fast to the pen. As her fingers worked, she surveyed the mixture of things left in the enclosure for the baby. The same doll and horse were present, but this time, instead of the crust of toast, there were several soda crackers lying in a flat pan. Meghan felt herself bristle at the sight.

"Like feeding a dog. Leaving you crackers in a tin pan. When I meet your mother, I'm definitely giving her a piece of my mind. New mother or not, she can't treat you like some animal to be caged and taken out at her convenience. Darn it to heck and back." She bit off the cuss words and grimaced at speaking them aloud with a baby in her arms. "Well, darn it," she said with a little less vengeance, "this just isn't right. And you know what, honey?" She nuzzled the baby's neck again, bringing forth a chuckle of delight from the child. "I'm going to stay right here until someone comes back."

"Like heck you are." The sound exploded through the cabin's open door.

Meghan whirled around, her heart jumping into her throat. Her fright transmitted itself to the baby, who jumped with her at the angry voice.

The tall figure standing in the doorway was shrouded in sunlight. All Meghan could make out was a silhouette, and that, in itself, was frightening. It filled the entire doorway.

She involuntarily squeezed the baby tighter to her chest, which resulted in a squeak of protest from the child. Sensing that all was not well, Rose began to cry.

"Now look what you've done." The words came out without conscious thought. Meghan felt some of her fear ebb, replaced by anger at the rude interruption. "Shh, shh, honey, it's okay." She jostled the baby up and down in her arms, a scowl on her face aimed at the bulk filling the doorway.

"What I've done?" the voice bellowed. "You've trespassed into my—"

"Will you be quiet!" Meghan interrupted. "Your cussing and bellowing aren't scaring anyone but this poor child."

"Give her to me." The angry demand was accompanied by action. The shadowy figure left the door and crossed the room in two paces.

Meghan's eyes widened as she took a few steps backward, only to bump up against the side of the pen. "I will not! I'm not letting go of her until her mother comes—certainly not to give her to a loud, demanding lout like you."

"Lady, I don't know who you are, but I don't make idle threats. If you don't hand her over, I'll—"

"You'll what?" Meghan's eyes shot blue sparks. Her face was flushed, and her hair itself sent a fiery warning to the tall man facing her. To Meghan, he seemed all chest and muscle. His wool shirt was rolled up, revealing sinewy forearms. Arms that were lightly tanned with a golden sprinkling of hair. But it was his face that held Meghan's gaze. His face and his eyes. They were a brown so dark, they seemed black now as anger and determination filled them. His lashes were thick and long, his face lean with prominent cheekbones, and his hair as dark as the bark of a walnut tree. He was the most beautiful and arresting man Meghan had ever seen, and she disliked him on sight.

"I'm not afraid of you, mister. And I intend to stay here until Rose's mother returns."

" 'Rose'? Lady, are you crazy? That baby you're squeezing so hard that you're scaring her is named Bonnie, not Rose. And if you're waiting until her mother returns, you'll have a mighty long wait."

"Bonnie?" she said, loosening her grip on the baby but still not relinquishing her to the man. "Fine, then. Bonnie. Since you seem to know so much, where is her mother?" Meghan's voice was cold, and sarcasm dripped from every word.

"Dead, but I doubt she's in heaven. Now give her here, and get out of my cabin." He grabbed Bonnie from Meghan and with strength and ease pulled the child against his chest.

Bonnie turned her head to look up at the man who had just snatched her away from Meghan's warmth, then smiled and took her two wet fingers and stuck them into the man's mouth. He bent his head and smiled at her. In that instant, he underwent a transformation. His black, angry eyes turned an amber brown as they filled with love for the tiny girl he held so securely in his arms.

The child gave a gurgle of delight and patted the side of his face with her other small hand, never taking the fingers from his mouth.

"I said, get out," he mumbled around the two fingers, directing a cold gaze at Meghan.

"If there's no mother, you must be . . ."

"Her father." He gently removed the baby's fingers from his mouth. "And, like I said, there is no mother, although what business of yours that is, I don't know."

The words were snarled, making Meghan stiffen her shoulder as she moved closer to the man. "It's my business when I find a child left alone in a pen. Fed like someone would feed a dog. Left with no one to look out after her needs, feed her, hold her, change her."

"So you're the one," he broke in. "You're the one who came in here the other day. That's twice you came uninvited into my home. How many other times, Miss Nosy?"

"Oh, nosy, am I? And what about you? What kind of father are you who leaves a baby alone, tied in a pen like some animal?"

"A father who has to work. A father who can't always take his child with him to do what has to be done. A father who can't find a decent woman to leave Bonnie with or a woman who's dependable. For the past few days the last woman I hired just didn't show up. I went looking for her this morning and found out she's up and left. No word, no warning." He looked down at the baby, his face reflecting his love. "I make sure I check on Bonnie every few hours. It's not what I want or planned, but sometimes life doesn't dish out what we plan. Anyway, she's safe. Look at her."

And with those words, he held Bonnie toward Meghan. "She's a lot better off than she was when her mother . . . Why am I explaining myself to you? It's none of your business, lady. What I do or don't do with my daughter is my concern, not yours. Now, I'm not going to ask again. Get out of my home."

Meghan stood, with her hands on her hips, eyes shooting sparks at the man. "I'm not leaving, Mr. . . ." She fumbled.

"Hendrickson. Conner Hendrickson. But that too is none of your business."

"As I said, or tried to say before your total lack of manners stopped me, I'm not leaving until I'm sure Bonnie is going to be all right."

Silence filled the room as the two antagonists faced each other, neither giving an inch.

Then it was broken by the sound of a small hand patting the man's face. Bonnie gurgled happily, then quickly leaned toward Meghan, her abrupt movement startling her father. Her small hands reached out.

Involuntarily Meghan stepped forward, only to pull herself up short at the warning scowl on the man's handsome face.

His eyes narrowed as he looked at his daughter, her hands reaching for the woman who was in his cabin, challenging him about the care of his own child. The muscles at the corners of his mouth jerked as he held back a smile. He was filled with reluctant admiration. This intruder was spunky. Not one bit afraid of him, and his size usually inspired, if not fear, respect in an opponent. And there was no doubt about it, she was his opponent.

"Bonnie will be all right. I've got somebody else lined up to come." The words were delivered with a little less anger. "I've managed to care for her up until now, and I don't see any reason I can't continue to do so. She and I do fine. We especially do fine without"—he curled up his lips—"a woman in the house. More than fine." He paused a minute to let his words settle in. "Now, Miss Nosy, don't you have somewhere to go? Someone else's business to stick your nose in? Because I've said all I intend to say to you other than, get out!"

Meghan took a deep, angry breath, turned her eyes to Bonnie and gave her a smile, then glared back at the man glaring at her. Her eyes were as cold as winter now as she stared into his face, her nostrils flared with suppressed anger. Then, without saying a word, she turned on her heel and strode across the room and out the door, shutting it with extra force behind her.

She was across the yard when she stopped short, thrust her hand into the deep pockets of her coat, and pulled out a muslin-wrapped package. With a set to her jaw and determination in every step, she quickly went back across the yard, up the steps, and slammed her palm against the door, sending it flying open. She crossed the room to the startled man standing where she'd left him just a few seconds ago and totally ignored him, looking only at Bonnie.

"Here's something I brought for you, honey." She

unwrapped the piece of muslin and held out one of its contents: a fat molasses cookie sprinkled with sugar crystals.

Bonnie needed no coaxing. A small hand shot out, grabbed the cookie, and knew immediately where to put it—into her waiting mouth.

Meghan turned and for the second time crossed the expanse of the room, pausing only long enough to lay the remaining contents of the muslin wrapper on the table. This time she closed the door with less of a vengeance.

The cabin was silent, the only movement that of the baby in the man's arms as she happily sucked on the cookie clutched in her hand.

Then a sigh of air left the man's body. "Well, I'll be darned. Bonnie, I don't know what wind just blew into our lives. No"—he smiled—"that wasn't a wind. That was a hurricane. Well, whatever it was, little gal"—he nuzzled the baby's cheek—"we don't need or want it, do we?" He crossed the floor and picked up the muslin package left on the table. He opened it and smiled at the contents.

"What the heck." He shrugged his wide shoulders and popped one of the fat cookies into his mouth.

Chapter Seven

Meghan fumed and muttered all the way home. She didn't notice the beauty of the fall colors, nor did the distance across the gulch seem as long. Her angry strides covered the ground quickly, punctuated by "Darn it to heck and back" every few feet. Meghan entered her snug home, threw her coat onto the bed, and slumped down in Granny's rocker. Angrily she set the chair moving.

"What a despicable person." The venom in her words filled the cabin. Enjoying the sound of her own voice saying aloud what she had been storing up on the way home, Meghan rocked even harder. "He's a bully, grabbing Bonnie out of my arms like that. And how dare he call me nosy? Huh!" she snorted. "Nosy, when all I did was go into his cabin and try to rescue his—his daughter. Nosy? Next time I'll . . ." She stopped her tirade.

There wouldn't be a next time.

70

She tried not to let the man's name-calling hurt her. "I've been called enough names without his starting it too. Well, it'll be a cold day in July before I'll go anywhere near that man. That's right, a cold day before I'll . . ." Then a thought hit her, and she felt a grin cross her face. "Before I'll trespass," she said weakly. Then she compressed her lips, trying to hold back the laughter that was bubbling up inside her as she replayed the earlier scene.

"Oh, my goodness," she mumbled with something akin to glee. "I was trespassing. Standing there in *his* cabin, yelling at *him*. Taking him on like a crazed badger."

An image of the surprised look on the man's face when she turned on him flashed into her mind, but it didn't hold a candle to the next image she saw—that of the man standing there, his jaw dropped, mouth open, when she'd barged back in the second time, slamming the door open, then marching over to hand Bonnie a cookie. She laughed. "His mouth was open so far, he'd catch flies if there were any."

She gave in to the freedom from anger the laughter was bringing as she replayed the day's events in her mind. Finally she wiped a tear from her eye, a smile still on her face, and whispered into the room, "Meghan, you do have a wicked temper."

She laughed aloud again. Then, slowing her rocking into a pleasant, lulling movement, she let her thoughts roam over the angry man and the impression he'd made on her. An impression that, up to this moment, she hadn't really acknowledged. Her heart seemed to speed up as she pictured his face, dark with anger, his eyes black as coal. She shook her head slowly, not liking the feeling this provoked. She rested against the high back of the rocker. Her last thought before the warmth of sleep seeped through her body and closed her eyes was of Bonnie and of the man. The man who had left her with no doubt of his love for his little girl. No, no doubt of his love, and no doubt of his anger.

The days rolled into a week, then two. Canning and preserving kept Meghan busy enough that she didn't think of little Bonnie Hendrickson as much during the day. But nights were a different story. She lay in bed, snuggled under her quilt, for the nights were getting cooler now, and, unbidden, thoughts of Bonnie crept into her mind. She worried about her. A couple of times she had ventured as far as the cabin yet had never crossed the clearing that led to the cabin's door. She had heard no cries from the cabin and took comfort from that fact.

Then, in the height of the busy canning and preserving season, a rash of colds took over the town. Meghan was much in demand, preparing her remedies of sage and spearmint tea to be used as a stimulant, making the pores of the skin open, increasing circulation, and promoting sweating. She favored catnip to gently relieve congestion. It was helpful with the children, especially when mixed with camomile and spearmint. A mixture of slippery-elm bark was soothing for scratchy throats. She brought her tins of goose grease to smear on chests tight with congestion. Hours were spent in the kitchen preparing a syrup of wild-cherry bark and honey for the numerous coughs.

Meghan's days were long, but each night, before she fell into an exhausted sleep, she thought of Bonnie. Was she doing okay? Was she far enough away from town, from other people, that she wouldn't be exposed to the germs? The thought of that tiny body hot with fever, her nose plugged with mucus, her chest tight as she fought the symptoms were enough to make Meghan want to cross the gulch and pound on the cabin door, demanding to see how Bonnie was, regardless of what her father decreed. She also thought, though she didn't want to admit it, of a pair of amber eyes set in an arrestingly handsome face. A face that stayed in her mind's eye, invading her thoughts when she least expected it.

She spent a few hours every day with Marybeth Phillips. They were becoming fast friends, and Meghan reveled in this, her first real friendship. But as close as she and Marybeth were becoming, Meghan never told her about Bonnie. And she certainly never told her about Bonnie's rude, angry father.

Meghan envied Marybeth her love for Emery, her son, and the unborn babe. She envied her the love that was returned from her "two special men," as they were referred to by the wife and mother. Yet, while she might envy their love and the closeness of the little family, Meghan didn't desire for one second to change places with Marybeth. The hardship her family was suffering, their lack of money to buy even the necessities, and the long, grueling hours Emery worked to make what little he did, was not something Meghan desired at all. At night, when she returned to her warm cabin, snug and safe, her pantry and root cellar stocked, her animals fed and securely penned, offering her security and independence, and the jars of money, untouched but waiting should they be needed, filled her with the joy of well-being and thankfulness. Her Granny had prepared well for her. She didn't need anyone else.

And when, at dusk, she sat alone at her table, gazing out over the spreading night, she pushed away the empty feeling that crept into her, working its way to her heart. And Meghan knew, though secure in her own home, wanting for naught, that she longed for something. While she couldn't give it a name, she knew it was the very thing cherished by her new friend, Marybeth.

Meghan sat at the table that evening, watching the night stealthily creep across the valley as silently as smoke. Night made itself known earlier now as fall deepened, and she savored each moment of the Indian summer. She was especially tired tonight. She'd been out since morning helping yet another new life make its way into Pig Eye Gulch. This time the baby came into a tent filled with several other children and a tired, dirty man who neither wanted nor welcomed another mouth to feed. The mother glanced at the baby, said she was glad it was a boy, not a bothersome girl, then fell into an exhausted sleep. Meghan had handed the tiny burden to a young girl standing there waiting for the bundle as if she knew this new addition to the family would be her responsibility, her task. She must have been no more than ten, yet there was already a tired oldness to her eyes as she looked unsmilingly at her new brother, then walked away from the bed where her mother lay and placed the babe in a wooden crate someone, probably this child woman, had padded with a ragged quilt. The hopelessness that permeated the tent home had filled Meghan with silent despair.

The older boy was one of the children who delighted in taunting her whenever possible. Meghan knew that the mother would not have sent for her had the labor not become overly long and the baby needed Meghan's help to coax it into this unwelcoming world. As soon as they no longer needed her assistance, the walls would close back around them, blocking her out, emphasizing again that she was an oddity in the small town. Needed but not fully accepted. Her knowledge and healing abilities branded her, so that, while the townspeople could not do without her services, they could easily shun her friendship. At least until they were forced by fate to admit her into their dismal lives.

Meghan never ceased to marvel at how short their memories ran. How easy it was to be grateful one day and to pretend she didn't exist the next. Granny had earned their respect, but she, Meghan, was still working for it. She thought the towns folk's trepidation was lessening. Lately she'd had been greeted with smiles from a few of the women, and they always found some way to pay her. How this family would, she didn't know, but they would—of that she had no doubt. Pride might be all they had left, but that they had aplenty.

She got up and set her cup in the basin. She arched her tired back and loosened her robe. It was earlier than her usual bedtime, but the day's toll, combined with the uneasiness inside, made her seek the comfort of her bed.

Walking to the range, she opened one of the lids and banked the coals with a small log. It would hold until morning, and there would be a bed of glowing embers to greet her when she put on the coffeepot to heat and perk, sending the aroma of fresh brew throughout the cabin, helping her welcome the morning and the new day. The thought made her smile. *I'll not pity myself any longer. I've so much. I've got a good life and now I've got a friend, Marybeth. Divine intervention sent me to her home. Not that I think God had anything to do with Jimmy's being burned.* A smile curved her lips as she thought of the yellow-haired little boy who stole into her heart more each day. The healing paste had worked. When the bandaging was removed, the blisters were re-absorbed, leaving only angry redness to heal. There would be scars, but they would fade as the child grew. And it was only the one arm. Meghan closed her eyes, thinking how much worse it could have been.

The small family had taken her into their lives, and she was becoming as familiar in their home as they were in hers. She saw less of Emery than of Marybeth and Jimmy. The young father worked twelve-hour shifts and often overtime if someone didn't show for a shift or extra work was offered. Emery's job involved partnering up for double-jack drilling in the solid rock of the mine. Part of the time he held the steel drill while his partner swung an eight-pound sledge against it. One slip and a man's hand would be mashed beyond use. Then they'd take turns, and Emery would swing the sledge, crouched and on bended knee in the tight spaces. Once they'd made a deep enough hole in the rock, they loaded it with dynamite. The load had to be just right—light enough to blast the rock loose but not so heavy as to bring it down on top of them. It was backbreaking and dangerous work. But they needed the money not only for living, but for their goal, the very reason they had left Colorado and traveled to Pig Eye Gulch to labor in the sapphire mines.

Their plan was to save every cent they could, and, when they had enough, they'd make a down payment on a piece of ground back in Colorado along the Colorado River. The land was rich and fertile, the climate mild. Fruit trees grew there with ease. The early springs and mild winters nurtured the trees that in spring graced the valley with umbrellas of showy blossoms and, in fall, yielded juicy peaches and pears. Emery would farm and give his family the life they deserved. By scrimping and saving every cent they could, they figured their dream would be a reality in two more years.

Meghan loved to hear them talk of Colorado, their stories of hot mineral springs bubbling up out of the ground and of outdoor bathing pools filled with the curious-smelling water. They told her she'd be especially interested in its healing properties. Many people came to the nearby town of Glenwood Springs to bathe in the pools and to partake of the mineral waters. She felt she would know the beautiful mountain town immediately and would be able to easily find her way along the river to the land they spent so many hours dreaming about. Meghan understood their love for Colorado and their desire to live there. She felt the same for the Big Snowy Mountains, the Judith Valley, and Pig Eye Gulch. *Didn't she?* Unbidden, the question popped into her mind. *Of course she did. She was just going through a strange time. A time of longing.*

Crossing to her dresser, she picked up her brush and began running it through her hair. The curls had tightened during the day, and she knew that if she didn't brush out the snarls, she would have a veritable rat's nest in the morning. Her hair crackled with each stroke as she pulled the brush through the resisting red strands. It sprung back with a life of fiery determination, willfully lying the way it wanted as it tumbled down her back. She blew out the lamp and was removing her robe when a loud, insistent pounding jarred the stout cabin door.

"Open up!" The shouted words were punctuated by another pummeling of fists against the wood. "Open up! A muffled curse was accompanied by what sounded like a boot kicking the bottom of the door. "I said, open up!"

Meghan felt her heart thump in her throat as she pulled the robe back up over her bare shoulders. The sash trailing as the robe billowed about her, she ran to the door as another wave of pounding shook it. She clutched the robe with one hand tightly against the hollow of her throat, while the other hand reached for the gun.

"What do you want?" Her voice rang out, each word

frosted with fear and anger. "I have a gun. I won't hesi-
tate to use it." She hoped the bravado with which she
delivered the last sentence wasn't lost on whoever was
using his fists to break down her door.

A disgusted curse was muffled, but the pounding
stopped.

"Listen, lady, I need you to open the door. I don't care
if you have a gun or not. I have a sick kid." He stopped,
waiting for a response. When there was none, the words
started again and were, if anything, louder and angrier,
though edged with sarcasm.

"Are you the uh, the"—he paused—"the woman who
heals? Look, lady, I don't know what you're called—
healer, witch, or whatever—and I don't care. But are you,
or aren't you? Standing here yelling through this door is
taking time. Time I don't have. Now, are you going to
open this door and help me, or am I going to break it
down? Because either way, you're going to—"

The words were cut off as the door flew open.

The man stepped back in surprise as a redheaded
wraith greeted him, standing at the end of a shotgun. Her
hair billowed out behind her as the light of his lantern
caught it in a glow of heat. Heat that was instantly doused
by her cold, piercing look. His quick intake of breath
was audible in the still of the night as took in her angry
beauty.

Then he sprang into action. He took a steellike grip of
her wrist, his long fingers easily circling it. He jerked her
to him in one forceful movement, causing her to stum-
ble as her bare feet flew across the porch. His other hand

grabbed up the lantern, and, without looking at her again, he pulled her across the porch and down the stairs, dragging her along behind him.

The gun fell from her hand as she thrashed, trying to stop her forward momentum. She doubled her hand into a fist and, throwing the weight of her rage into it, pummeled the side of his face, catching his lower lip. She felt it mash against his teeth.

His head snapped back, and he dropped her hand, releasing her from his painful grip. "Are you crazy, lady? What's the matter with you?" He scowled as he rubbed his bruised lip, the tip of his tongue gently testing the cut corner of his mouth.

Meghan's breath was coming in gasps, one hand gripping the top of her robe, the other curled into a fist at her side.

" 'What's the matter with you? Are you crazy?' " Each word came out in a gasp of air. "How dare you manhandle me like that, you big . . ." She searched for a vile-enough word. "Oh, darn it to heck and back." She threw her favorite epithet at the man.

The man's face was hidden by the night. She had yet to see him full on, but something about him seemed familiar. Then he held the lantern up.

"Oh!" Her gasp filled the distance between them. "Mr. Hendrickson. I didn't realize it was you. I never saw your face."

"You only hit people you know?" he growled, rubbing his jaw.

"Of course not! I'm so sorry." Then she stopped as the

memory of his rough handling flooded through her. "I take that back. I'm not sorry. Do you always grab women out of their homes, Mr. Hendrickson? After you've all but kicked in their door, I might add?" She reached for the ties of her robe and with more force than necessary belted it around her waist. "I'm hardly dressed for a night's outing," she mumbled. "I don't know the reason for your rude, arrogant, boorish behavior, but . . ."

Setting the lantern down in the path, Connar looked at the woman facing him, her anger making her all the more beautiful and vibrant. Then he swooped her up into his arms, crushing her against his hard chest, turned around, and started back up the steps into her cabin.

"If you'll just shut up and give me a second, I'll repeat what I said earlier." The words came through a clenched jaw.

Meghan pursed her lips. She couldn't have spoken if she'd wanted to. There wasn't enough air in her, so tightly was she held. She could feel Hendrickson's heart pounding through the heavy fabric of his shirt.

He hit the cabin door with one shoulder and stepped into the darkened room. He looked around, then caught sight of her lantern.

"I'm going to put you down, but I don't have time to play games or put up with any nonsense from you, do you understand?"

"Mr. Hendrickson, this is my home, and you cannot—"

"Do you understand?" he roared, his breath warm on her face. "I'm not going to hurt you. I need you. Anyway,

I hope you're the one I need. If not, I've wasted a lot of valuable time. Now, do we have an understanding?"

Meghan nodded as he lowered her until her bare feet touched the cabin floor. Still he didn't release her. One arm circled her waist, and for a second it was as if he'd forgotten his mission, his reason for rousting her so forcefully from her home. Then he let her go and quickly turned away. He removed the chimney from her lantern, and within seconds a bright glow filled the cabin. Now she clearly saw his face. She closed her eyes in embarrassment at the bright streak of blood at one side of his mouth. His lip was beginning to puff, and she knew it was cut on the inside. Well, darn it, he shouldn't have been such a bully. How was she to know who was pounding so rudely on her door?

Watching him deftly trim the lantern's wick, she felt herself grow warm as she gazed at his handsome profile. She could feel his arms as though they were still around her. There had been the smell of the night and autumn about him. She had felt an unprecedented feeling of security while there in his arms, a safe sense of coming home.

"Are you the healer?" His words startled her as he turned to face her. "They gave me the name of a Meghan O'Reiley and directed me to this cabin. Is that you?"

She was unable to form an answer quickly enough to answer him before he started talking again.

"Answer me," he ordered. "Because if you aren't, I've wasted too much time." His black brows tightened over his dark eyes. A muscle at the side of his face jerked with the effort he was making to restrain himself from yelling.

"I am Meghan O'Reiley. And yes, Mr. Hendrickson, I am trained in healing." She spoke the words quietly, emphasizing each one.

"Bonnie's sick."

The words sent a chill through Meghan as she pictured the sweet baby.

"Mr. Hendrickson, you will have to do better than that. What exactly do you mean by 'sick'? I'm not just idly curious. I have to know what herbs to bring with me."

The man took a deep breath, willing himself to have the patience needed to explain Bonnie's symptoms.

"She feels hot. She hasn't eaten much for the past two days. She cries constantly. I haven't been able to work; she screams when I put her down." He flushed as he gave the next symptom. "And she has runny bowels. You know . . ."

"Yes, Mr. Hendrickson, I do know. Go on."

"That's about all. Oh, yes, she drools."

"Drools?"

"Yes, her mouth. Drools."

"Ah." Meghan's eyes lit up. "I think I know what's wrong, Mr. Hendrickson."

"You do?"

"Yes. Of course, I need to accompany you to your cabin and see for myself. However, I would like to get there on my own power without your generous assistance." She scowled at him.

He gave a slight shake of his head as an embarrassed

frown crossed his face. "I'm sorry. I left her crying in that pen, and I had a heck of a time finding this place. Every moment away from her in this condition scares me. Look, could we finish this conversation later? Right now I want nothing more than to escort you"—he smiled at the word—"back to Bonnie. Would you please grab whatever you need so we can go?"

Meghan didn't answer. Instead she went to her cupboard and started pulling out jars of herbs. "Do you have any—no, I suppose you wouldn't," she said, answering her own question. She reached for a small container of rendered goose fat and added it to the growing pile of supplies on the table.

He stood there watching her as she efficiently compiled what she seemed to know was needed.

"I'm ready." She picked up the canvas bag of supplies, only to have it taken from her hands.

"I'll carry it. You get your shoes on and"—his eyes twinkled—"you might consider wearing something besides your nightgown. Hate to create any more talk."

Meghan stopped short. "Turn around, Mr. Hendrickson," she said tersely.

Feeling awkward taking off her robe with a man only a few feet away, Meghan first pulled on the trousers she'd made just for occasions like this. Gingerly she slid her robe and gown up over her head and quickly put on a heavy shirt. The night air would be cool, but her wool vest would protest her. Finally she reached for her high-topped moccasins.

"You can turn around now, Mr. Hendrickson. I'm just about ready."

He looked at her, then scowled as he looked at the footwear she was pulling on.

"What are those?"

"Moccasins. Don't worry. I can go anywhere you can go in your boots." She gave a final jerk to the laces and straightened up. "Didn't you say you left Bonnie crying?"

"Yes." His answer was short, his cold mask back in place. "Keep up with me. I'm sure you remember the way to my cabin," he said sarcastically as he opened the door and plunged into the night.

Chapter Eight

Meghan heard Bonnie before she reached the cabin. The man a few paces in front of her broke into a run, covering the few feet to the door in seconds. He was reaching into the pen, lifting up the sobbing baby, when she entered the room.

"Let me have her, Mr. Hendrickson." She reached for the baby, not expecting nor receiving any resistance. Murmuring soft words of comfort, she laid the baby on the only bed in the room. She took off her vest and bumped into the father, standing mere inches behind her.

"Please, Mr. Hendrickson. I need room to work and breathe. You would be of more help if you made some hot water available. I'm going to check Bonnie over from head to toe, but, as I said earlier, I think I know what her problem is. If I'm right, it's not serious."

"How could you know so quickly? You've hardly

touched her. I don't believe in witches, but maybe you are one." The words were softly spoken, and the twinkle in his eye belied the insult. There was even a hint of admiration in his voice. "I'll check the stove and see that the teakettle is full. Anything else?"

"I'll let you know." He was already dismissed and out of her mind. Her focus was on the baby fretfully sucking on two fingers. Meghan's hands roamed over the small form, touching here and there.

Picking the baby up, she smiled at the sounds coming from the kitchen. Stove lids banged, and something hit the floor with a thud, accompanied by a growling curse.

Carrying the baby into the kitchen, Meghan once again saw the bond between baby and father. Bonnie leaned toward him, letting him know she wasn't happy at all. Meghan handed the baby into his waiting arms. He patted her back as he gently rocked her.

"It's just as I thought. I'll mix a few things, and I think we can get Miss Bonnie quieted down. Maybe even get her a good night's sleep." She smiled. "And maybe one for her dad too. You look exhausted, Mr. Hendrickson."

"That's neither here nor there. What's wrong with her?"

"She's teething."

"Teething?"

"Yep. A couple of front teeth are ready to pop through. See?" She gently lowered the baby's lower lip. "These swollen bumps are covering two little teeth."

Bonnie turned her head away, burying it in her daddy's chest, rubbing it back and forth across his shirt.

"You're wrong. This can't be normal. Her gums are red and twice the size they should be. She's feverish. Maybe I ought to bundle her up and head for Lewistown or Great Falls. One of them should have a doctor."

"That's up to you, of course. And I'd encourage you to do just that if you want to put Bonnie through more misery than she's already in and if you want to look darn foolish. Bonnie's a healthy little girl, and she's simply having a hard time doing what nature has planned for her to do. But, like I said, it's up to you." Meghan tilted her head and looked him in the eye. She made her face as blank as possible, hoping he would respond to her indifference. She sensed that Conner Hendrickson wouldn't take well to anyone pushing him in any direction but his own.

"You sure?" he asked suspiciously.

"I'm sure."

"Well, it's dark now," he mumbled more to himself than her. "Okay. I'll give you until morning to do what you seem to think you can do. But if she's not one heck of a lot better, I'm taking her to Lewistown. Like I said, if I have to, I'll go on to Great Falls."

"Mr. Hendrickson, you do have a way about you. I just don't know how to thank you for the privilege of being rousted out of my home to be so eloquently shown your appreciation and confidence." She picked up her sack and began unloading its contents. She missed the flash of his smile. "And as long as we're on the subject of your eloquence, my name is Meghan, not *lady*."

"Okay, fair enough. Mine's Conner. Darn!" He quickly

moved Bonnie. A large wet spot was forming on the front of his shirt. He turned his head away at the smell hovering over the little girl and him.

"Loose bowels, Conner?" she asked sweetly.

He narrowed his eyes. "Don't enjoy this too much, lad—uh, Meghan. I've about run out of diapers, and that creek is getting colder each day."

"You're washing them in the creek? No wonder they're so gray. It's a miracle she doesn't have a diaper rash on top of everything thing else." She stopped and looked at the flush on his face as he turned his back, taking Bonnie to the bed for changing. "She does, doesn't she?"

"Does what?" came the muffled response.

"Have a diaper rash."

"Maybe. Yeah. Yes, her bottom's red. Happy?"

"Not at all, and Bonnie isn't either."

As if agreeing, Bonnie raised her cries even louder.

Meghan shook her head. Then all talk stopped as both adults went to work, one putting together the healing herbs and the other gingerly removing a smelly diaper.

Meghan reached for an iron skillet hanging on a wall. "Do you have any flour, Conner?"

"Flour?"

"Yes, and don't fasten up that diaper yet. Leave it off for a few minutes so air can hit that sore bottom while I get together something to help heal her."

"Leave it off? Leave her naked?"

"Yes," she chuckled. "Naked as the day she was born. Now, where's the flour?"

"In that big tin beside the cupboard." He motioned with his head.

Meghan took the lid off the tin and, using a large spoon, scooped out flour and put it into the warmed skillet, stirring as it turned a light brown.

She was unaware that she was humming softly to herself. Conner watched the woman's sure movements.

Meghan scraped the flour into a bowl and ran the substance through her fingers to cool it. "You can apply this to Bonnie's bottom." She handed the bowl to Conner.

He looked askance at the bowl, then at her. "You expect me to put brown flour on her?"

"Yes, I do. Browned flour works wonders healing diaper rash. Pat it all over her bottom every time you change her. Between your not boiling her diapers after you rinse them in the creek, and her cutting teeth, she stands the chance of having a rash that will be difficult to heal if we don't get on it now."

He heard the word *we* and the lonely, helpless feeling that often engulfed him was momentarily stilled. He hoped the woman was right and that nothing more serious than cutting teeth was ailing Bonnie.

He left the baby on the bed, where she fretfully kicked her bare legs and chewed on her knuckles, and he stood in the doorway watching Meghan work. He turned so he could keep a watchful eye on the baby and yet see the woman.

Meghan quietly murmured each ingredient, much like an incantation, as she mixed them in her wooden bowl. "First crush the cloves. Then, when the heated goose grease melts to an oil, add the crushed cloves and steep for about five minutes. Strain through a clean cloth. That should make enough clove oil to rub on her gums."

"You're mumbling."

"What?" A perplexed frown crossed Meghan's brow. "Here." She handed him the oil. "Rub this on Bonnie's gums. But not too much or too often. Try it." He dipped a finger into the oil and, walking over to the baby, hesitantly rubbed her swollen gums. Bonnie stopped her fussing and held completely still, enjoying the soothing feel of the oil.

"To answer your remark about my *mumbling*"—she emphasized the word—"when Granny taught me, she always made me recite the entire process aloud. I guess the habit stuck."

"Your granny taught you the art of healing?" He suddenly realized he wanted to know more about this unusual woman who seemed to have taken over his cabin.

"Yes. I'm not as good as she was, but no one could have had a better teacher. I grew up watching and listening as Granny used herbs and common sense to take care of the people in this valley. I don't think there was much of anything that could stump her." Meghan's voice was filled with love and admiration.

"You don't live with her. I didn't see anyone else in your cabin."

"No, she's dead. I lost her a few years ago. I did live with her in that same cabin, though. She left it to me, along with whatever knowledge she could impart. I'm not ignorant, Conner. She also saw that I was educated, though no amount of schooling could equal what I learned from that amazing woman."

"She sounds amazing," he said wistfully. "It must be wonderful to have had someone that special in your life." His voice drifted off, but not before Meghan heard the sad longing in it. She focused again on the task at hand, not wanting to make him uncomfortable. They seemed to have reached a quiet understanding, and Meghan didn't want to do anything to disturb that. She had no doubt that, if she couldn't soothe Bonnie, quiet understanding or not, he would take the baby to Lewistown at first light.

"I'm going to mix some flaxseed in water for Bonnie's bottle. It should help check that diarrhea. It'll look thick and squishy, but don't worry about that—she'll like it. Don't add honey to sweeten it—that just might add to the problem. Although it's really not uncommon for her bowels to be runny while teething, I'd be sure to boil her bottles and any water you give her. You can probably look forward to more days like this until she's through teething." This was delivered over her shoulder as she filled the bottle with the grayish substance.

"Now," she said, picking up a bottle of oil and going over to the bed, "this is extract of lobelia. I'm going to rub some on Bonnie. You can go ahead and diaper her." She stood to one side and watched as he patted on the brown flour, then, with only a slight awkwardness, securely pinned the diaper. The crying had stopped as well as most of the baby's fretful movements.

Under the father's watchful eye, she turned the baby

over onto her stomach, then applied a small amount of oil to the tiny spine. Using a circular motion, she rubbed the oil into the child's back.

"Is this where she sleeps?" she quietly asked.

"No," he whispered. "She has her own bed, but don't move her. If she falls asleep, I don't want to disturb her. There's not enough night left for me to try to get any sleep before I have to leave for work in the morning."

Meghan smiled sympathetically as she continued rubbing. "You must work in the mines like everybody here does. Well, not everybody," she said, thinking of the few store owners. "But the sapphire mines support just about everybody one way or another, if you can call some of their meager existence *support*." She thought sadly of Emery and Marybeth. "It's too bad you've had to miss work. I don't suppose the owner is very sympathetic. And then there's the money loss." She wasn't looking at the man as she spoke. She was intent on what she was doing.

"Uh, yes. The money," he muttered as he looked away. He picked up the bottle. "Doesn't look like she'll need this. She's almost asleep." His voice was low, his surprise evident.

"Still doubtful, Conner?" Meghan asked as she gently pulled a blanket up over the sleeping baby.

"Watchful," came the tired reply.

"Why don't you go sit in that chair, or, better yet, lie down beside Bonnie. I'll straighten up my mess."

"Chair's fine. I'll just sit down while you're doing whatever you have to do, then I'll walk you back to your cabin." He shook his head, smiling. "She sure looks peaceful. Nothing like the little screaming banshee I've had on my hands the last few days. What do I do if she wakes up?"

"Rub her gums with the oil of cloves. Give her the bottle of flaxseed if she'll take it, and if she's fretful at all, rub her back with the lobelia, starting at the base of her spine."

"I don't know how to thank you," he said, all threats of Lewistown seemingly forgotten. "I'll see that you are compensated." He lowered himself into the chair and laid his head against the back. "Bonnie is everything to me." His voice dwindled off as his eyes shut, and sleep quickly overtook him.

Meghan stood there a few minutes watching the exhausted man. She'd pack her things and then take herself back to her cabin. She'd traveled this valley many nights in situations similar to this. She knew her way and knew that, occasionally ridiculed as she might be, she was grudgingly respected around here. No one would harm her. She glanced over at the sleeping baby, small and content in the big bed, then back at the man. Placing everything back in her sack, she put her vest on and quietly opened the door. It was hard to leave. But she'd done what she'd been asked to do. She'd played a minor role in their lives. Now it was over. So why was it so hard to leave the cabin and the sleeping baby? And the sleeping man. Why was it hard to leave him?

Chapter Nine

Morning came early, but not as early as it likely had for Conner. Meghan quietly pushed the cabin door open, expecting to find the baby and Conner still sleeping. The stars were slowly fading from the sky as she entered and realized she'd been half right. Bonnie was still asleep, and if it wasn't that she was sleeping now in her pen, Meghan would have sworn she hadn't moved all night. Her small mouth was making sucking movements, and Meghan figured she'd wake up hungry and wet at any moment.

She glanced around the room and saw the evidence that Conner had been up and busy. There was moistness in the air, and the reason for it was draped over every available surface. Diapers had been rinsed and boiled. There were also two empty bottles draining on a towel by the sink. Propped against one of the bottles was a note. Meghan anxiously reached for it.

Meghan, I knew you'd come at first light to check on Bonnie, so I left early for work. Mrs. Wilson has been hired to look after Bonnie, and so far she's been dependable. She knows to come early, but I'll look in on Bonnie every few hours. If she doesn't show, I'll stay with her. I put a bottle of the stuff you mixed up beside her in case she wakes up before you arrive. We'll be fine now. Like I said, I'll see that you're compensated.

Her smile faded to a frown by the time she finished reading. It was a note of thanks and dismissal. Well, what did she expect? She'd do what she needed to do, make Bonnie comfortable and then leave. The baby was her father's responsibility, and it was plain that that was what he expected. Again, she was an outsider looking in. Whatever made her think this time would be any different?

The heavy feeling didn't lift as she mixed more oil and browned more flour. She wanted to leave enough to get Conner through the next few weeks of Bonnie's teething. She still felt low when, later that morning, after greeting and instructing Mrs. Wilson, she closed the door and left the happy baby playing.

Unanswered questions followed her home. Why was Conner so bitter about Bonnie's mother? Why didn't he mourn her death? Why was Conner caring for a small baby all by himself? Was there no family to help? And why was he in Pig Eye Gulch working in a sapphire mine? He didn't seem the type. In fact, he spoke as though educated and with a certain polish and confidence about him. Life had beaten on him, but he wasn't as beaten down as many of the men in this valley were. These were all questions she had no right to ask and no right to expect answered.

During the following weeks, Meghan tried to put Conner and Bonnie Hendrickson out of her mind. She chastised herself whenever she caught herself thinking of him. Against her will, the tall, angry man had made an impression. She could close her eyes and see his face as various emotions moved across it. Anger certainly, but also love, love for his baby girl. She admired him for shouldering the tremendous responsibility of working, caring for a baby, and making a home. Working in the mines was dangerous. And while the locals claimed this valley's sapphire mine was safer and better run than some of the others, a man still took his life in his hands every time he climbed into the sinking bucket and was lowered into the shaft. But what else was there? The sapphire mine was the lifeblood of Pig Eye Gulch. The mine seemed to be a better provider for Conner than it was for many of the other miners. He had a cabin, and while it wasn't huge, it was a big improvement over much of the other housing in the valley. He had to work long hours, yet he didn't seem as drawn and sallow as the others. He seemed to manage work and yet could check on the baby during the day. How he accomplished this was certainly a puzzle, but it was none of her business.

Meghan carefully placed some eggs into a basket along with some carrots and acorn squash from her garden. The big brown eggs would be most welcome at Roberts' General Store, where she hoped to trade them for some flannel. Marybeth's baby wasn't too far off, and she wanted to surprise her with a couple of night-gowns for the new infant. She combed her hair and tied a bright green ribbon around it. Meghan used to enjoy going into the general store stocked with its many items ranging from groceries to dry goods. And she still did enjoy it when Mr. Roberts was gone and Mrs. Roberts waited on customers. When he was there alone, Meghan felt uncomfortable from the minute she entered the store until she left. She found that if she planned her trips for Wednesdays, Mrs. Roberts would be there. Though not overly friendly, at least the woman left her alone to shop. Today she looked forward to browsing through the shelves and tables of merchandise. She knew Marybeth was secretly hoping for a little girl, and the last time she was in the store, she'd seen a bolt of light pink flannel. It would be perfect for a small gown, with maybe some ribbon for trim. If there was time, she would embroider roses around the neck line and hem. The autumn sun fell warm on her shoulders, and the thought of doing something for her friend filled her with pleasure.

Meghan stepped into the doorway and was announced by the clanging of the cowbell hanging over it. The place was empty, and she assumed Mrs. Roberts was in the back. She placed her basket on the wide counter and went to the table with the bolt of flannel. It was just as soft and pretty as she remembered it. Pink and perfect for a little girl.

Her hand was rubbing the soft fabric when she felt a warm breath on the back of her neck.

"You sure look pretty today, Meghan."

Meghan spun around. "Mr. Roberts," she said, stepping back.

"Those are mighty fine-lookin' eggs and vegetables." He motioned toward the counter.

Meghan swallowed hard, "Uh, is Mrs. Roberts here? I usually deal with her."

"Well, no, Meghan. She had a real unexpected errand to run. Somethin' I needed her to do today. But I'd be pleased to help you." He took a step forward as she took a matching step back.

Meghan felt her back touch the wall and knew she had no way to escape the advancing man. Her mouth was dry, and her heart beat in her throat.

"You seem to be favorin' that bolt of material there."

"Yes." Looking up at the man, she tried to act as though nothing was amiss.

"I'd be glad to cut you off some. Waiting on a pretty customer like you is a real pleasure, Meghan." He moved even closer, trapping her. Leaning forward, he rested one arm against the wall and let one finger idly stroke her cheek.

"Mr. Roberts, I've . . . I've changed my mind. I don't want . . . please move, Mr. Roberts. Please."

The man grinned, ignoring her discomfort and the fear in her eyes.

"Is there a problem, Meghan?" The question was posed in a cold, harsh tone.

Mr. Roberts quickly dropped his arm. The grin left his face, to be replaced by a sickly smile as he turned toward the voice.

"No, no problem. No problem at all," he answered. "I'm"—he gulped hard, his Adam's apple bobbing— "I'm just helping Meghan here with a purchase. Isn't that right, Meghan?"

Conner Hendrickson reached around the stammering man and pulled Meghan to him. "That wasn't what it looked like to me." His eyes narrowed at the shopkeeper.

Meghan offered no resistance to his arm resting protectively around her shoulders.

"No, honest, Mr. Hendrickson. Why, I've known Meghan for a long time. A real long time. Watched her grow up. Knew her granny." The man sputtered out the words, but his voice was full of respect.

"Uh-huh. Well, you see, Mr. Roberts, Miss O'Reiley is a friend of mine. I'd just naturally expect she be treated with all the courtesy a woman deserves. In fact, I'd be mighty upset, as I'm sure your wife would be, if Miss O'Reiley ever mentioned that you were inappropriate in any action. Even more, Mr. Roberts, I'd be mighty upset if even your tone of voice was the least bit disrespectful to her. I just might have to see about doing trade somewhere else. You might be the only general store in Pig Eye Gulch, but another one just might spring up, and wouldn't that be a shame? All your business going to a new store?"

"Oh, no, sir, Mr. Hendrickson. No need to think that

way. No need, uh-uh, no need. Why, I'm proud to have Meghan . . ."

"*Miss* Meghan, Mr. Roberts." There was steel in the correction.

"Oh. Right. Miss Meghan, as a customer. Yes, sir, I'll see that she is treated with all the courtesy due her."

"I'm sure you will, Mr. Roberts. Still, you might want to be sure Mrs. Roberts is the person to help Miss Meghan in the future. Of course, should she not be here, Miss O'Reiley would have no reason to be afraid to come into the store to trade with you, would she?"

"No reason at all, Mr. Hendrickson. No reason at all. Why, I was just getting to tradin' Megha . . . Miss Meghan's basket there on the counter for some of that material she was admirin.' "

"That right, Meghan?" He looked down at her, his smile gentle.

Meghan licked her lips. "Yes, I wanted to get enough to make my friend a gown for her expected baby." Her voice was a whisper echoing in the too-quiet store.

"You go right ahead and get what you need. I'm sure Mr. Roberts will make you a very fair trade." He arched his eyebrows at the man.

Mr. Roberts turned so sharply as he grabbed up the bolt of material, he bumped his hip into the counter—hard. Not pausing one moment to acknowledge the pain, he took the fabric to the counter and began unrolling the bolt.

"Need anything else, Meghan?" Conner Hendrickson asked softly.

She looked up at him, feeling drawn into the darkness of his eyes. "Thank you." She whispered words only he could hear.

He nodded. "Get whatever else you need. You won't be bothered again. I'll wait for you by the door."

Meghan gathered up the thread and ribbon she wanted for the gown. She had to force herself to concentrate; the joy in shopping she'd felt earlier had evaporated. She picked out four small buttons from a jar and added them to her other items on the counter. Mr. Roberts worked quickly, avoiding her eyes, asking only how much fabric she wanted. He was very respectful and businesslike. Meghan couldn't help smiling. She'd never been waited on with such courtesy.

Mr. Roberts wrapped the purchases in brown paper and tied it with string. He offered it to Meghan, but it was taken from his hands by Conner.

"Does that seem like a fair trade for those fresh eggs and vegetables, Meghan?" Conner asked.

"I . . . I guess."

"I believe in all fairness to Miss Meghan—and I do believe in being fair—she has a small credit left," Mr. Roberts piped in, a greasy smile creasing his face. "Was there anything else you were wantin', Miss Meghan, or would you like that credit put on the books?"

"On the books, I suppose, Mr. Roberts. I've never had credit over anything I've brought in, although I know Granny often did. Yes, credit would be fine," she said. For the first time, she faced the odious man with complete confidence.

The sun was bright as she and Conner walked out, leaving to stammerings of "Thank you" and "Glad to have your business."

They walked in silence. At the shade of an old cottonwood tree on the edge of the town, Meghan stopped.

"I don't know how to thank you." She shook her head, her eyes moist with emotion. "I'm afraid I was in a very precarious position. I always shop on Wednesday when Mrs. Roberts is there. I never would have gone into the store had I known she was out on an errand."

"I'm sure he knew that. I have no doubt that old devil made darn sure she'd be out most of the day. When I saw him touching you, I wanted to beat him to a pulp. He thought he could get away with making advances because you're alone with no one to protect you." His angry words spilled out, his fists clenched, as he recalled the scene. "Well, right decision or not, he won't bother you again. I want you to promise me that if he or any other man makes advances or makes you uncomfortable in any way, you'll tell me. Promise me, Meghan," he said forcefully.

"I promise," she said quietly. "I promise, Conner. And consider me well compensated for anything I did for Bonnie." He started to shake his head no. "Yes. What you did today—well, I don't know what I would have done had you not happened to come along when you did. I am more than paid."

"Look, Meghan, I don't take favors. Especially from a, well, from anyone," he finished lamely.

"You meant to say from a woman, didn't you?"

He shrugged. "Here." He held out an envelope.

"What is it?"

"Payment."

"Mr. Hendrickson." The warmth was gone from her voice. "I did something for you. You did something for me. I consider us even. Now, if you'll excuse me, I have other things to do."

He turned away with a muffled oath, then went a few feet and stopped. "Truth is, I didn't just happen along." The words were spoken over his shoulder. "I went to your cabin first. I took a chance you were in town and knew the general store would be the only place you'd frequent. The timing was right."

"You went to my cabin? Is Bonnie all right?" Anger forgotten, she retraced her steps until she faced him.

"Yes, I went to your cabin. And, yes, Bonnie is all right. More than all right. She has two fine teeth that just shine when she smiles, which is a lot more often lately. She looks like a little rabbit, but darn if they aren't pretty."

"How precious," Meghan said, her voice tender. "I would like to see them."

He went still. Then he put the envelope back into his pocket and said, "Uh, well, that probably could be arranged. Would you like to have dinner with Bonnie and me?"

"Dinner?"

"Yes. You needn't be concerned. I make a fair stew."

"I'm sure you do, but are you sure, Mr. Hendrickson? I don't want you to feel obligated in any way."

"I don't. And, no, I'm not sure. But come anyway. You might enjoy a night off from cooking and eating alone. And I might enjoy the company. One thing's for certain, those two little teeth are an incentive to come, now aren't they?"

"Well"—she chuckled—"it's not the most gracious invitation I've ever received, but I'll take you up on it. I'd love to come. When?"

"Tomorrow? I won't be working in the afternoon, so I'll have plenty of time to prepare the stew. That is, I should have plenty of time if Miss Bonnie will cooperate. She's getting to be more of a handful each day. I'm afraid my daughter is going to be a very determined young lady. And darned if I don't see signs of a real temper."

"Tomorrow would be fine. Can I bring anything?"

"Nope. It won't be grand, but it will be filling. Why don't you come over at about five? That should give you time to look your patient over and admire those teeth."

"I'll be there." Amazingly, the sunshine had come back into Meghan. "Thank you again. Thank you for everything. Tell Bonnie her guest can hardly wait." And with steps a great deal lighter, she started up the path to her cabin.

"Very definitely I'll be there," she said to herself. "Very definitely."

Chapter Ten

It seemed to Meghan that minutes were boulders, so slowly did they move. She set out many tasks to accomplish, hoping to make the time move more quickly. It didn't work. By noon she'd finished everything she'd set out to do. The third time she looked at the clock, she threw up her hands, muttered under her breath, and decided to go outside and pull some of the determined weeds constantly invading her garden. It was her least enjoyed chore, but maybe the hoeing and bending would take her mind off tonight. She told herself she was looking forward to the dinner invitation because of Bonnie. And, while she was looking forward to seeing the baby girl and her new teeth, that was by no means the only reason. Conner. She was drawn to him, deny it as she might. Perhaps tonight he would feel comfortable enough with her to open the door to his life just a crack, just enough to let her know more of the man inside.

Weeding was an excellent choice. The hard work made the time pass a little quicker, and by three o'clock she put the hoe away, exchanging it for the washtub hanging outside the woodshed's door. Carrying it into the kitchen, she filled it, emptying the range's reservoir of hot water. Then she sprinkled some powdered lilac into the water and inhaled deeply the sweet, pungent odor. Lowering herself in, she let her thoughts float to the evening ahead. Tonight would be a first for Meghan. Oh, she'd been invited to dinner before, but never by a man, and especially not a man like Conner Hendrickson.

Meghan spent extra time with her hair, then slipped on the deep blue gown she'd worn to various school functions. She'd had no occasion to wear it since leaving school, and she'd forgotten how the blue taffeta shimmered and changed colors in the light. It was the perfect companion for the fiery highlights in her hair. She chuckled at the rugged contrast her moccasins made and decided she'd put her soft leather shoes into a bag and slip them on just before she got to Conner's. Satisfied, she shut the cabin door behind her and made her way to the evening ahead.

By the time she reached the cabin, her anticipation had changed from excitement to apprehension. What if Conner regretted asking her? What if they found nothing in common to talk about and the evening dragged with embarrassing emptiness? He'd asked her not as a guest but as someone he needed to repay for a night's help with his daughter. She cautioned herself not to read more into the invitation than the man meant. She slipped on her shoes and smoothed a hand down the front of her dress. Maybe she was overdressed. She should have stayed with her everyday calico or cotton prints. She should have refused the invitation. What had she been thinking? "Okay, Meghan," she chided. "As Granny would say, the fat's in the fire. You've no choice but to go forward."

Conner, baby in arms, answered her timid knock. The first words out of his mouth did little to lay to rest all her fears and questions. "You're early. Come in." He stepped back, and she stepped into a room full of warmth and redolent aromas.

"Something smells good," she said with a smile and a glance at a large pot simmering on the back of the range.

"Yeah," he said. "I told you I made a mean pot of stew. I can also fry an egg and make a pan of oatmeal."

"Really? And after that?"

"And after that"—he laughed—"you're on your own. So far I've been lucky. Bonnie likes oatmeal. However, I think I'd better add mashed potatoes and gravy to my can-do list. This girl will be wanting to try out those new teeth." He turned the baby to her, and Bonnie gave a happy gurgle, and, without coaxing, leaned toward Meghan.

"Oh, my," Meghan said, reaching out, "those are pretty teeth, Bonnie." She snuggled the baby under her chin, then whispered to her, "You gave your daddy quite a scare. I don't think I've seen a grown man more upset. And all over two little bumps in your mouth."

" 'Little bumps,' my foot," he growled. "I'll have you know those two little bumps had me walking the floor with a screaming baby for two days before I came for you. Now, Miss Meghan, you'd better sit down here at this table and behave before I decide to eat all this stew myself. You can put the naughty lady in your arms into that chair there. I'll tie a dishcloth around her and the ladder-back. That should hold her."

"Why don't you put a potato and some vegetables from the stew on a plate to cool? I'll mash them all together, and we'll see what Mistress Bonnie thinks of your cooking."

"You think that's a good idea? I mean, is she ready? She still has her bottle." He gave her a worried frown. "It's just that I don't want . . ."

"You don't want her to have fresh vegetables? Sorry, Conner, but this young lady is a growing girl, and growing girls need more than milk. She's ready, so, Dad, quit fussing like a mother hen." Meghan laughed as she chided the worried man.

"Okay, but if she gets sick, you'll be the one rousted out of bed to tend to her."

"Oh, I don't doubt that."

Meghan put the baby on the chair seat and held her while Conner tied the towel around her small waist. They accomplished the task as if they had always been partners in caring for the baby.

Bonnie sat upright, enjoying her new independence.

Meghan reached for a spoon beside one of the dishes and handed it to the baby. She noticed the beautiful place settings and glanced at Conner, his back to her as he lifted the pot off the stove. Running her fingers over the gold-trimmed rim of the delicate plate, she gently picked it up. *Limoges*. The word was stamped on the bottom of the plate. She quickly put it back down. Conner stood there, pot in hand.

"I, uh, I was just admiring . . ."

"Wedding present." The words were terse. He set the stew on the table and took up her plate, ladling out the appetizing meat, potatoes, and vegetables.

All was silence as both adults tried to ignore the sudden awkwardness.

"This looks good, Conner." Meghan spoke softly.

"Thank you." Relieved, he smiled at her. "Well, do you want to have the pleasure of offering Bonnie the first bite, or shall I?"

"You. I'll watch and give excellent advice."

"Okay, here goes. Look here, Bonnie. See what Daddy made? Stew. Lots of nice vegetables that Meghan thinks you need." He risked a teasing glance in Meghan's direction, the spoon hovering near Bonnie's mouth.

Bonnie's hand flew up and with a quick swipe batted the spoon, flinging potatoes, vegetables, and broth down the front of Conner's shirt.

He jumped back, his surprised movement bringing forth giggles of delight from the baby and a peal of laughter from Meghan.

"You think this is funny, do you?" he said, attempting

a menacing look. Bonnie clearly thought her daddy was funny, and Meghan was thoroughly enjoying him too.

"Okay, Miss Expert, your turn. Let's see you get the spoon into the mouth." He handed it to Meghan and stepped back, a knowing smile on his face.

Meghan took the spoon and dipped it into the cooled mixture, then gently placed the tip of the spoon at the side of Bonnie's mouth. The small mouth automatically responded to the pressure and opened wide, taking in the spoon, contents and all.

"That's my girl! Pretty good, huh?" Meghan crooned.

Bonnie rolled the food around in her mouth, her blue eyes wide as she explored the taste and texture. "Mmm," she hummed, letting some of the broth dribble down her small chin.

"You little traitor, you," Conner muttered as he picked up a dishcloth and wiped her mouth. "Not fair, Miss Meghan. You've done this before."

"Yep. A few times. Nice shirt, Mr. Hendrickson. Several pretty colors," Meghan said as he wiped at the mess there.

"I'd stop there if I were you," he warned, the warmth of his voice taking away any threat.

"Pooh, you don't scare me, Mr. Hendrickson. I've seen what a little girl can do to you. You're too easy." She plopped another spoonful into Bonnie's waiting mouth.

"Eat. You're the guest of honor. I'll feed the naughty lady." He took the spoon from her hand, his fingers lightly brushing hers.

The touch danced through him, taking him by surprise. Time stopped.

Conner's eyes darkened with something Meghan couldn't define. He had taken her breath away with a single touch.

They both turned toward the baby to defuse the electricity in the air.

The rest of the meal was spent in relaxed, easy banter. Bonnie ate most of the food on her plate, then began spitting out anything else offered.

"Want to take Bonnie and change her out of that mess she's wearing? I'll clear the table. The dishes can wait until later."

"Of course not, Conner. I'll help. We can have them done in no time."

"Nope. You're the guest, remember? There's a clean gown on the table beside the bed. Diapers too. Believe me, Meghan, one night of not having to wrestle that wiggle-worm into her nightgown is more of a treat than help with dishes."

"I'd love nothing more than to wrestle this cutie pie." She picked up the messy baby and gingerly held her away as she carried her to the bed.

Conner was filled with the rightness of the moment and wondered if this special woman, with her gift of healing, could heal *him*? The protective barrier he'd built around himself would have to dissolve first. He turned from the two of them and began clearing the table.

Chapter Eleven

The evening sprouted wings and flew. They had another cup of coffee, another snuggle of the baby girl, and another discussion on teething. The cabin filled with their talk, their laughter, and comfortable silences. But the one thing they didn't do, the one thing Conner was unable to do, was to talk about him. Every time he started, the words twisted on his tongue, and the hard lump in his stomach moved up to his throat. If Meghan noticed, she gave no sign.

Conner did learn more about the woman and the granny who had almost tripped over her as a baby left on her doorstep. He was caught up in her stories and could almost see the child who only wanted to run barefoot in her mountain valley.

She told him of her last days at Miss Fairchild's. As Meghan spoke, he felt a fierce protectiveness in him, and he knew he'd fight tigers before he'd let anyone . hurt Bonnie the way Meghan had been hurt.

Meghan stopped midsentence and glanced out the small window. "Oh, my gosh, I didn't realize it was so late. I'm afraid I've overstayed my welcome. I know you've got to get up early for work." Megan's face flushed, and she rose to her feet, taking her vest off the back of a chair. "I don't know what came over me except that you are such a good listener. I haven't talked so much about myself since . . . you know, I don't think I ever have." She cocked her head.

"Stop," he said. "If it wasn't getting dark earlier, we'd have time for another cup of coffee and another story or two. I wish I'd known your granny."

"Me, too. Granny would have loved Bonnie. And she would have thought you very handsome and dashing."

A red flush crept up his neck. "What do you think?"

It was her turn to be at a loss for words, her turn to feel the flush of embarrassment. "Me, well, I think . . . I think it's time for me to go home. I've had a lovely evening. Thank you for asking me.

"I don't like your going alone on these trails when it's close to dark. Let me put Bonnie into her pen and at least walk you halfway."

"I know these mountain trails like the back of my hand. But I need to go while it's still twilight. Kiss Bonnie good-bye for me, will you? And, Conner, next time it's your turn."

"My turn?" he asked, perplexed.

"Yes, your turn. I'll cook, you come, and I'll listen

while you talk. I suddenly realized I didn't hear one thing tonight about Conner Hendrickson."

"Maybe there's not that much to hear."

Her voice softened, and her eyes held a special light. "I don't believe that for a moment."

"Go, but be careful, Meghan."

Meghan was out the door and halfway home before his last words played through her mind with enough force that she stopped in her tracks. "My Meghan," she said aloud to the night. "He called me, my Meghan. I wonder if he realized what he said?" But her heart told her what her mind wanted to question: that Conner Hendrickson was the type of man who always knew exactly what he was saying. She wrapped that thought around her like a blanket, using it to keep her warm not only the rest of way home but for the days that followed.

Meghan fought with herself not to seek out Conner the next day and invite him and Bonnie over for dinner. "Give it a few days, Meghan," she chided herself. "You don't want to appear overeager." But she was eager. She found herself humming more as she went about her chores, and even the bothersome antics of the few boys who just couldn't give up using her as an outlet for their excess energy seemed less annoying. She was able to repeat to herself what Granny probably would have said regarding them. *"Meghan, don't be such a worrywart. Boys will be boys."*

It was a beautiful Indian summer day, and she was out in the chicken pen when she thought she saw movement along the edge of the creek bank. There, she saw it again, a shadow moving in and out of the trees. She stepped back to where she was partially hidden by the chicken house and yet able to see. Quietly she waited. The autumn sun warmed her shoulders as the mountain waited with her, quiet with the fall's silently changing leaves. Her patience was rewarded. It was a boy, bent over, slipping from tree to tree, his movements as furtive as the looks he cast over his shoulder. Meghan was unable to see who it was until, gaining confidence, he stood still in an opening, head cocked, listening. She didn't know his name merely as one of the boys who enjoyed plaguing her with jeers and pinecones. He was also the same boy who'd stood outside the tent, unable to face her, the night his mother gave birth to yet another boy.

Meghan waited until he was out of sight. Then she took off on moccasined feet, tracking him off the trail and into a copse of trees. She heard murmuring coming from deep within the foliage. The words were unclear, but the voice drifting back was filled with soothing calmness. She slipped closer. There he was, crouched before a small makeshift shelter that looked as if it had been put together by someone attempting to weave branches. There were gaps in the structure, and branches protruded every which way. The boy kneeling before it was so caught up in comforting whatever was inside the makeshift cave, he was oblivious to anything or anyone around him. The object of his deep concentration wasn't visible to anyone but him.

Meghan edged closer to listen.

"Don't worry, girl. I told you I wouldn't let anyone hurt you. Told you I'd be back today. Brought you something to eat. Not much, but we ain't got much left over after we all eat. I slipped this into my pocket from my breakfast. You like pancakes? Wish I had me some meat. Bet you'd really like that. You need meat so's you can keep nursing your baby. I tore the pancake into little pieces. Slow down. Ma'd be real mad if she know I snuck any food outta the tent. Says we got too many mouths to feed and she don't know why the good Lord seed fit to give her yet another." His next words were spoken more to himself. "She's got a baby too, but I don't think she likes it as much as you like yours. You lick yours, but Ma hardly never does more'n feed and change hers. She sure don't kiss him none." The next words were quieter. "She don't kiss none of us anymore. Pa don't neither." The voice stopped, and all was quiet. Then a hesitant giggle came from the trees, followed by another and yet another.

Meghan crept closer, putting one foot softly down in front of the other. She was hardly breathing. She pulled back a branch, smiling at the tender sight greeting her. Sitting back on his heels, a small puff of fur in his hands, his face buried in it, was the boy. Lying there closely watching him was a brown, shaggy mongrel. Its coat was dull, and Meghan was sure she could count every rib.

The instant the dog saw her, the hair at the ruff of its neck rose, and it emitted a low, warning growl. The boy whirled around, his eyes large in his thin face.

Meghan dropped to her knees, doing her best not to appear threatening. "I'm sorry to disturb you," she whispered to the boy and dog. "I . . . I saw you, and"—she shrugged apologetically—"I followed you. Please don't be angry. Your secret's safe with me."

"Yeah?" His one word was filled with distrust and skepticism. "I'll bet. Why would you care?"

"Because I love animals too," Meghan said, and she leaned closer to him. "Puppy's not very old," she said.

"'Bout a week," he said, and she heard the pride in his voice. Meghan wondered how many meals he'd shorted himself so he could share with the mother dog.

"Just one?"

"Yep. Had another, but it died. This one, though, he's tough. I'm gonna call him Scrapper." He looked at Meghan as if daring her to contradict him.

"That's a good name," she said softly, and a tentative touch accompanied her words as she her fingertips grazed the soft mound of fur held protectively in the boy's hands.

"You ain't telling for real?"

"For real. But I'd like to help."

His next words were spoken with suspicion and all the wisdom of someone who had little reason to trust adults. "Ain't agreein' to nuthin.'" He waited a minute; then curiosity got the best of him. "Exactly what would I be agreein' to?"

"Well," she said, looking fully into his blue eyes, "I'd like to be your partner in caring for these two."

Meghan glanced toward the mother dog, lying there alert and watchful. Seeing the boy's discomfort at her words, she hurried on. "What I mean is, you would own the two dogs, mother and puppy, but I would feed and shelter them."

"Why would you do that? You don't owe me nothin'. I ain't been real friendly-like to you." He squared his thin shoulders and waited.

"This isn't for you; it's for this mama dog and her baby. They're going to need more and more food as the baby grows, and they'll need a little bit better home with winter coming."

The boy slowly nodded, reluctant yet smart enough to know that what she said was true.

"So," Meghan said, holding her fingers out to the mother dog to sniff, "what do you think?" The dog sniffed. Then she lowered her head, allowing Meghan to, with the lightest of touches, stroke her.

The boy watched her, and, like the dog, he knew Meghan would keep her word. He knew, too, that the dogs needed more than he could give them. It would be only a matter of time before he was caught sneaking scraps, only a matter of time before autumn would give way to winter's strength. Snow would come to the mountains, and tree-snapping cold. He looked at the mother dog as if searching for guidance. Then he looked back at Meghan, his face pinched.

"She ain't yours. And neither is the puppy." His eyes narrowed, daring her to argue.

Meghan hesitated only a second, then held out her hand. "Deal." She smiled. "Partner."

He slipped his small, rough hand into hers and then squeezed her fingers with a firm grip.

"You know," Meghan said, "since we're going to be partners, don't you think I should know your name? Mine's Meghan."

"I know." He lowered his eyes for a second, remembering how he'd just the other day yelled taunting words at her. "Mine's Jeremy. Jeremy Burke."

"Well, Jeremy Burke, I'm pleased to meet you. And I'm pleased to be your partner. Now, we've got some decisions to make. How do you feel about moving . . . say, what is her name? Have you given her one?"

He shook his head. "No, I can't find one that fits. I thought maybe Spot, 'cept she don't have any. *Fearless* is a boy's name, isn't it?" He looked at Meghan, clearly hoping she'd disagree and maybe say Fearless sounded just right.

"Well . . ." Meghan said drawing the word out. "*Fearless* sure would fit her, but I agree with you—it's more masculine, and she's definitely a lady." The dog leaned into her hand, enjoying Meghan's fingers now stroking down her head and back, stopping to scratch behind one matted ear. "That's it. Jeremy, that's it!" she exclaimed.

"What?"

"That's her name, and you knew it all along."

"I . . . I did?"

"Yes, you as much said so. You knew she was a lady dog. . . ."

"Anybody would, uh, know that," he said.

"Let's call her Lady. What do you think?" Meghan's enthusiasm was infectious.

"Lady," he said hesitantly, then with more conviction in his voice, "Lady. Yeah, Lady. Sure, that's good, and I really did know that, even if you said it 'fore I did."

Meghan took her hand from the dog's back and ruffled the boy's hair. "Jeremy, what would you say to our leaving Lady here for just a little while? I have an empty corner in my woodshed I think would make a warm home, but I'll need your help getting it ready. Do you need to get permission or let someone know where you are? I don't want you getting into trouble or worrying your mom."

"Naw. I done all my chores. Usually my friends and I mess around until near dinnertime. Then for sure I got to get home. I'm in charge of getting my little brother washed up, and my sister does the new baby. Ma gets real mad if we ain't there. We gonna move her tonight?"

"I'd sure like to. She'd be a lot more comfortable and safer too. And maybe I can find her a little more to eat. She looks like she's missed quite a few meals."

"She used to belong to a family that lived here up until a few weeks ago. They up and moved to Lewistown. Their dad said there was more gold there and he could make more money. My dad thought of going too 'cept he likes working here. Dad says money's nice in Lewistown, and, boy, we sure do need it, but this mine's a lot safer. He says the owner seems like a real stand-up guy and is trying to change things, so he thinks we'll try and stick it out."

The partnership seemed to have loosened Jeremy's tongue, and he gave Meghan an even deeper look into his family and their lives.

"Then it's settled. You put Scrapper back with his mother, and you and I will fix up their home and hurry back so we can move them before you have to leave. You know, I think I just might have some chocolate cake left. I baked one yesterday, and there's only me to eat it. You probably don't like chocolate cake. . . ."

"I do," he broke in excitedly, his eyes shining with delight at the prospect. "I sure do, ma'am."

"Meghan. Please call me Meghan. We're partners, so it's okay."

"Okay, Meghan. I'd be real pleased to help you eat some of that cake. Real pleased." Jeremy grinned.

Chapter Twelve

Two pieces of chocolate cake later, a cozy dog bed was made in the woodshed. There would be plenty of room for the small canine family.

"Well, Jeremy," Meghan asked, "are you and I are strong enough to get Lady and Scrapper loaded into this garden wagon?"

His small chest puffed out. "Sure. I'm plenty strong enough. How about I pull it 'til we get there?"

Meghan could see he wanted nothing more than to get his hands on the wagon. "Sounds good to me. I'll just follow along. I put a few pieces of cornbread from my supper last night into a rag, just in case we have to coax her."

The boy looked at her, his face a study in perplexity. "You aren't so bad. What I mean is," he stammered, his face flushed and freckles popping out, "for a girl, that is. My dad would probably say you're real stand-up too."

"I would consider that a nice compliment, Jeremy. I'm glad we're partners."

"Me too. Say, you wouldn't happen to have any more of that cake you aren't wantin'? I'd sure like to take my sister a piece. She won't believe me when I tell her how good it was."

Meghan laughed. "Well, you know, I do believe I have another piece. Remind me to give it to you when we get Lady back here and settled."

"I won't forget."

Meghan smiled. There was no doubt in her mind. The cake had gone a long way toward sealing the partnership.

It was late afternoon by the time they'd convinced Lady to cooperate with the move to her new home, a lot of pulling and pushing before they got her into the wagon. Despite Jeremy's claim of being strong, Meghan found the dog had a mind of her own, and it didn't involve riding in a wagon. Without the cornbread, Meghan doubted the move could have been accomplished.

Standing back, the partners finally surveyed the day's work. Lady and Scrapper lay side by side on a soft quilt. Meghan had promised the mother something more than cornbread for her supper. Chocolate cake in hand—a piece for his sister and the rest of the cake to share as he desired—Jeremy was ready to leave for home.

"Uh, Meghan, you gonna mind if I come see them?" He still wasn't sure of the new relationship.

"Of course not. Anytime. They're yours, aren't they?"

"Well, yeah, 'cept now they're part yours."

"Jeremy, even if I'm not home, you can come see them. Spend as much time as you want. During the warm days I'll leave the door open so they can come in and out and enjoy the sunshine. Of course, Scrapper won't be able to go anywhere until he gets a lot bigger. But the way he's eating, I don't think that will take very long." She chuckled as she rubbed the sleeping pup's tummy. Lady, her head resting between crossed paws, looked as if she were anxious for them to leave so she could get on with the important business of checking out her new home and comfy quilt.

Meghan followed Jeremy out of the shed and watched as he trudged down the mountain path toward home. Today had been a good day, and she had made a new friend. "And I've increased my family by two," she murmured, feeling happy as she contemplated long winter nights with two canine companions helping to ease the loneliness that, with unsuspecting stealth, crept in.

The next day she was feeding Lady and holding the warm pup when she heard her name being called.

"Meghan. Meghan, you home?"

She jumped up, a smile on her face. *Conner.*

"I'm in the woodshed. Come here and see what I've got." Her face was wreathed in a smile as she watched the handsome man approach.

"Hey, that's some pup." His voice was soft as he reached for the curled ball of fur. "Where did you find him?"

"Well, actually, I didn't find him. Jeremy did."

"Jeremy," he said, losing the smile. "Who's Jeremy?"

She laughed, delighted with his response. "A ten-year-old boy with freckles."

Two dimples etched the sides of his mouth as the smile reappeared. "Ten years old, huh?"

"Yep."

"With freckles?"

"And a passion for chocolate cake." Standing closely, they both took turns petting the pup, and she told him about yesterday's adventure. "So," she concluded, "we're partners. He owns the two, and I provide room and board."

"Sounds like you were taken, lady." He reached over and gave her hair a tweak, his hand savoring the silkiness of the curl.

Meghan didn't answer. She couldn't. When she finally found her voice, she asked, "Did you need something, Conner?"

"Hmm?"

"Did you need something?" she repeated.

"Oh, yeah." He blinked. "I'm going to be gone for a few days."

"Gone?" she asked, her voice weak.

"Some business I have to take care of in Helena. I just wanted you to know so you wouldn't come with that dinner invitation and no one there to accept it," he said teasingly.

She took the puppy from his hand and, fighting disappointment, opened the door and stepped inside the shed. Conner watched as she carefully put the pup back alongside its mother, who was eyeing yet another stranger, not sure if he was friend or foe.

"You think she'd let me pet her?" he asked as he lowered himself to his heels.

"Sure," Meghan answered, patting the dog's head, "she's a sweetie. I think she's grateful to have a warm, safe place and enough to eat. She seems to really enjoy company. Her name's Lady."

"Well, Lady, looks like you have a pretty good situation here." He gently scratched her head.

"When will you be back?" Meghan asked.

"Two, maybe three days. I'm taking Bonnie, of course. She needs a few things, and this is a good chance to buy ahead for the winter. Is there anything I can bring you back?"

You, she wanted to say, but instead she shook her head. "No, I think I've got everything I need."

"Meghan, I've been doing a lot of thinking since our dinner. There's something we need to talk about when I get back." His tone was serious. "Something I want to share with you." Seeing the questioning look on her face, he said, "Curiosity will make you look forward to my return. A little anticipation is good for the soul, don't you think?"

"No." She laughed. "I don't think. Now I'll wonder the entire time you're gone." The silence stretched between them, eloquent with unsaid words.

Then Conner got to his feet, slowly and reluctantly. "I'd better go. I've got a lot to do before I leave tomorrow." He opened the door and went outside, shutting it gently behind him, not trusting himself to stay in the close confines of the shed any longer. Meghan was becoming much too important to him. How had this happened to him? He who was so sure that no woman would ever mean enough to evoke those strong feelings. And he'd been just as sure no woman would ever pierce the protective wall he'd built around him and Bonnie. Those were thoughts and realizations he'd have to explore more fully when he could think clearly—without the baffling emotions whirling inside. He was dreading the few days away from Meghan, and he promised himself that when he returned, he'd do something about the aching loneliness that had invaded him since he'd met the feisty redhead.

Meghan stood looking at the closed door, biting her lower lip, willing away the emptiness. She glanced down at the mother dog and was already appreciating her companionship. Giving a sigh, she started toward the door, when her foot brushed against a piece of paper wedged between the quilt and the dog. Bending down, she picked it up and unfolded the page. She read the first few sentences before she realized it was a letter. A letter to Conner. It must have fallen out of his pocket as he crouched to pet the dog. She didn't mean to—she really didn't—but her eyes followed the scratchy penmanship with a will of their own.

Dear Conner,

Well, son, it sounds as if you were right, and the mine can be made profitable. Selling it to you was the best business decision I made. Still, your mother and I wish

*you would change your mind and come home to Eng-
land. We miss you and little Bonnie.*

Meghan closed her eyes, and with a heavy heart she
quickly opened the door and ran to the path leading into
the town. She could see Conner's back, and she called
out his name. She paused, then called it again, louder this
time.

He stopped, then turned around. Meghan stood at the
top of the path waving the piece of paper. His forehead
wrinkled in puzzlement, and he started back up the way
he'd come.

"That curious huh,?" he teased as he neared her. "Now
what would Granny say about that? 'Curiosity killed the
cat'?" He paused, seeing the troubled look on her face.

"You must have dropped this." She held out the letter.

Conner took it from her and slowly opened it, glancing at the words. He folded it, looked off into the distance for a moment, then in a tired voice said, "We need
to talk."

"No, please, I have no right . . . you owe me no explanation. I owe you an apology, but I only read enough to
know it was yours. It must have fallen out of your pocket
as you pet Lady." Her face flushed.

"Meghan," he said. He took her arm and turned her toward the cabin, "I may not owe you an explanation, but I
want to give you one. Could we go inside and sit down?"

She nodded and opened the cabin door. "Would you
like a cup of coffee?" she asked, stalling for time. She realized she didn't know Conner Hendrickson at all. She'd
thought he worked in the mine, but apparently he didn't.

He owned it. She'd been so naïve, sharing with him stories of her modest upbringing, when just a few lines of the letter bespoke his more affluent circumstances.

She took down two cups and filled them with the coffee simmering on the back of the stove. "It's only a few hours old," she offered, setting a cup in front of him.

"Thank you." He sensed her discomfort and felt it himself. "Sit down, Meghan. I don't talk much about myself. I've gotten out of the habit of sharing my life, and I've been guilty of letting you believe—well, I've let you believe me to be something I'm not. Please." His eyes were dark with unsaid words.

Meghan slid into the chair facing him and wrapped her hands around her cup.

"You might as well hear it all. I tried to tell you some of this when I had you over for dinner, but the night was so perfect, I didn't want to ruin it. You're the first woman since—" He took a deep breath and plunged on. "I'm getting ahead of myself. I'd better start from the beginning."

"Conner, you don't have to tell me anything. I'm embarrassed that I mistook you for a working man, dependent on the mine and losing time from work when Bonnie was teething. I wish I could take it all back." She closed her eyes for a second, then opened them to gaze into her coffee cup, as if the solution to this awkward moment could be found there.

"Meghan," he said softly, "I thought you sweet to be so concerned. I wanted to correct you, but I also wanted to be what you thought I was: an ordinary man who needed the help of a gifted, beautiful woman." He waited for a response from her, took a deep breath, and searched for the right words.

Then he resolutely began his story. "I am a miner, but I don't work in the mine. I own it. My father owns two the larger ones, and he sold me this one in Pig Eye Gulch. I love my father dearly, but we don't always see eye-to-eye on mining issues. Thanks to my education, I've more progressive thoughts and ways of mining. He's coming along, and, as he said in the letter, he's now glad he sold the mine to me. It wasn't always that way."

His voice lowered in reflection, and Meghan sensed there had been troubled moments between the two.

"I left home in anger and vowed I'd never go back to England, not even for a visit. Anger's a terrible thing, Meghan." His eyes implored her for understanding.

Her heart went out to him, but she was hurt. Hurt by his lies of omission.

"Yes, we're wealthy. My mother is an American heiress. It's through her influence that I am more American than English. I always had an American nanny and tutor. I got my formal education in America." He gave a small shrug. "That's why I have no accent.

"My father has been quite successful with his mines both in England and here. I grew up hearing him talk of this valley and the beautiful Yogo sapphires. I knew that I would come here someday and be a part of bringing those stones to light. As I got older and learned more about mining, I knew I also wanted to make changes, try some new techniques. My father and I quarreled. Finally, with my mother's influence, he agreed to sell me one of the mines. But by then harsh words had been spoken, and I left England angry.

His next words were so low, Meghan had to strain to hear them.

"As I said, I left England, but I didn't leave alone." He raised his head and looked at her, his eyes sad and with a faraway look. "I left with a wife that my father and mother disapproved of. They thought her a fortune hunter. And you know what, Meghan?"

She shook her head.

"They were right." Resolutely he went on with the story. "She hated Pig Eye Gulch. She hated not having a grand house. She hated the mines and the good people working in them. She hated being with child, hated having her figure ruined, hated being clumsy as her time came closer. And in the end, she hated me."

He shook his head at the painful memories. "Don't get me wrong. It wasn't all her fault. I was so wrapped up in my mine and in proving my father wrong, I didn't pay enough attention to her. I missed all the warning signals. I truly didn't realize how miserable she was and how badly she hated her new life."

He pushed the coffee cup away. "Bonnie was born." His frown softened at the memory. "I had me a beautiful baby girl. One look at her, and I was filled with a love I'd never experienced. My wife felt even more left out and resented the baby. We hired woman after woman, but none pleased her. I tried to help—I really did—but the mine was a jealous mistress, and I gave it the majority of my time and thought."

He took a deep breath and squared his shoulders. "I came home one day to find Bonnie alone in the cabin. She was wet and smelly. Her bottle was soured, so I knew she'd been alone for some time. She was so tiny, Meghan. So tiny and so helpless. I was all thumbs, but I somehow got her changed and fed. There was a letter on the kitchen table, and I waited until Bonnie was asleep before I opened it and read what I'd suspected all along. She'd left me and Bonnie."

He stopped talking and looked at her. "Not a pretty story, huh? Well, it's almost over, and then I'll leave."

His words cut through her like a knife. But before she could offer any words of consolation or protest, he took up the unhappy tale again.

"She was returning to England, the letter read. Going back to her family, her friends, and her more exciting life. Back to where people knew how to have a good time. She didn't want the baby—I could have her. But what she did want was my money—lots of it." He shrugged. "I gave it to her. But I got the better deal. I got Bonnie. My father came through for me and took care of the legalities. We would remain married but live separately. I would keep our child, and I would give my wife a lump sum of money and then more each month." He smiled ruefully. "She had expensive tastes and wanted the lifestyle she'd thought marrying me would provide. My parents were right: She was a gold digger."

He paused and looked at Meghan for a response, some acknowledgment of all just he'd shared with her.

"You're married." The accusation fell loudly in the silent room.

"No, I didn't lie to you about that. She's dead. A carriage accident a year ago. And, yes, I'm bitter. I'd lost any feelings for her. Leaving me, I could try to understand, but leaving our precious daughter for . . . for money and fun? That I never could forgive. Like I said," he continued, his voice harsh and cold, "I don't mourn her, and I seriously doubt she's in heaven."

Then, in a different tone, he said, "Bonnie and I do fine. Our cabin is cozy. However, lately I've started wanting a real home. I was going to start having one built when I first arrived in Pig Eye Gulch, but after my wife left, that desire left also."

"I'm sorry for you." These words fell as softly as snow.

"Don't be. Bonnie and I are far better off. And I'm learning as she grows. We've made it through teething, thanks to you, and we'll make it through anything else life throws at us. But"—he paused and looked at her— "I'm beginning to wonder if I do need to open the door just a crack, just wide enough to let someone else in. I swore I'd never let myself trust or love another woman. I swore I didn't need anyone, but maybe I do. Maybe I do," he repeated. Then he slowly got to his feet.

"Meghan, I've dropped a lot on you just now. I don't expect you to understand, but I hope you do. I wasn't deliberately misleading you."

"I know you weren't. Thank you for sharing what

had to be hard for you to share. Right now I'm at a loss for words."

"Meghan, I would have spared you all this, but . . . you've invaded my thoughts, and"—his voice lowered—"I've found myself picturing you being a part of Bonnie's and my life. I wanted to be open and honest with you about everything, but"—he shrugged "I needed more time. This—you—it's all been so sudden."

She followed him to the door, lost and bewildered by the turn the afternoon had taken. She was casting around for the right words to say when he turned back to her, hand on the door latch.

"As I said earlier, I'll be gone for a few days. I've dreaded going, but now I think it's for the best. Maybe . . ." He left the sentence unfinished. "Good-bye, Meghan. Take care of yourself and your 'partner.' "

"Good-bye," she whispered as she closed the door on the man she suddenly realized she loved.

Chapter Thirteen

The autumn sun shone everywhere but in Meghan's heart. She counted the days until Conner would return and she could say the words she wished she had said the day he left. Ever since that day she had been plagued with what Granny would have called the "if only's." *If only* she had said she understood. *If only* she had told him she didn't blame him for his wife leaving him. *If only* she had said how proud she was of him for being a kind and loving father and how lucky Bonnie was to have him. And the biggest *if only* of all: *If only* she had told him how she felt about him. But she couldn't. She simply couldn't. She wondered if she ever would be able to share her feelings.

"No, I won't," she said aloud to the stillness of the room. "We come from different worlds. And"—she took a deep breath—"this valley is alive because of him and his mine. The people here depend on him. Conner deserves someone comfortable in his world, not someone like me, who feels more at home with herbs, animals, and healing than with a big, fancy house and all the entertainments that go with it. And surely he will go back to England someday." Someday he and Bonnie would no longer be content in Pig Eye Gulch. And someday Conner would step out of her life just as suddenly as he'd slipped into it.

She shook her head, trying to rid it of the black thoughts. She took off her apron and hung it on a hook by the sink. She would devote no more of the day to worrying about tomorrow. *"Kid, sometimes the best solution to a worrisome problem is the dawning of a new day,"* she could almost hear Granny say. *"Things always look brighter and easier to bear come morning and a new day in this beautiful valley. Why, I just put my problems in a dresser drawer and don't pull them out until I'm wearin' my next day's clothes."*

"Granny," she softly said, "I'm going to do just that. And," she added with a twinkle in her eye, "I'm going to put my hands to work. You always said idle hands make the devil's work, and I think mine have been idle long enough. I have too much to be thankful for and too many blessings to count. I've got friends, both human and animal." She thought fondly of the two dogs in the woodshed, one of them waiting patiently for breakfast and becoming more trusting. "I just wish you were here to enjoy all this with me, Granny. And, darn it to heck and back, I wish you were here to size up Conner like only you could do."

Today, she decided, was the day to start on several projects that needed completing. First, she would go check on Marybeth. Her baby was due in about a month, and she seemed overly tired. Meghan tried to help with Jimmy as much as possible in the hope that Marybeth could sit down, put her feet up, and steal a few minutes of rest. Meghan had mixed her an evening tea of oat grass, lemon balm, and chamomile to sip before bedtime, hoping the herbs would relax her enough to get a peaceful night's rest. Still, she reminded herself, Marybeth was certainly in good spirits.

Meghan smiled. Marybeth was so sure this baby would be a girl. She hoped she was right, because if not, there would be a baby boy wearing a soft pink flannel gown with delicate embroidered roses.

Thinking of the gown made her remember the day she'd bought the material, and like so many things had done of late, that made her think of Conner. It seemed as if suddenly everything in her life held a tiny memory of him.

"Back into the drawer with you," she admonished, chuckling at the fanciful image the words conjured up.

She pushed the teakettle to the back of the stove and, opening a lid, banked the coals. There was nothing worse than coming home to a cold, unwelcoming stove. She paused in her chore when she heard someone calling from outside. Before she could investigate, there was a knock on the door. Opening it, she was faced with a homely, red-faced, young man, ears sprouting out like the handles on a jug. His hair, a shock of yellow straw, stood straight up. His clothes were clean but patched, and he seemed to be having difficulty raising his eyes to her face.

"Hello. May I help you?"

"Yes'm. You're the her . . . her . . . herb lady, ain't you?" he said.

"Yes," she said hesitantly. "I'm the herb lady." And she offered a reassuring smile.

"Ma asks real po-lite if you would come and bring your herbs. We have need of your services." He slowly recited the sentences, pronouncing each word as if he'd had to repeat them several times before being trusted with the message.

"Yes, of course I'll come. But who's sick?"

"No one."

"No one?" she asked, puzzled.

"Nope."

"I'm sorry, I guess I don't understand. Your mother is asking me to come and bring my herbs, but no one's sick."

"Yep."

Meghan slowly shook her head, brow wrinkled. The messenger peered at her as if she was a disappointment for not being bright enough to understand a message that seemed perfectly clear to him.

She took a deep breath, then smiled.

"O-kay," she said, drawing out the word. "Let me make sure I've got this right. You need me to come." His head bobbed up and down. "But no one's sick." More head bobbing, and this time he gave her a proud look much as that of a teacher to a pupil who had finally managed to get something right. "What's the matter? What is the ailment, the problem?" she asked lamely.

"Milk looks like water. An' she's swollen some. Red too."

At last. Meghan gave a sigh of thanks. Now they were getting somewhere. She only had a few more questions, and she'd know exactly what to bring with her.

"How old's the baby?"

"Don't have one yet."

"No baby?"

"Nope."

"There's milk but no baby?"

"Yep."

Meghan gave a deep sigh of exasperation. They were back to one-word answers.

"What's your name?" She had to have at least one sensible answer.

"First or last?"

"Oh, dear," she said aloud. "First."

"Stanley."

"Last?" Now she was starting to sound like him.

"Black."

"Okay, Stanley Black. Let's try again."

"Okay, ma'am. But Ma said for me to not play around. I was to get you and come right back."

"I understand. And believe me, Stanley, that's just what I want to do. "Milk's watery, she's swollen some, and is red. There's no baby. Uh, Stanley, could you tell me how much milk she's leaking?"

"Leakin'? Ain't never heard it called leakin'."

"Stanley." She was trying to keep the exasperation from her voice. "You said there's no baby. When did she have her last baby?"

"'Bout two years ago, but it ain't here no more if you're wantin' to see it. It was a real cute one though, ma'am. Sure hated to kill it, but Ma said we had to— that's what they're for."

Meghan felt her head swim, and she prayed for divine assistance. "Why," she asked weakly, not sure she wanted to know the answer, "why did you kill it? Stanley, why?"

"Cause, Ma said we had to." He was getting as frustrated as she was. Hadn't he already told her that Ma said that's what they were for?

"You had to," she repeated weakly, feeling the need to sit down.

"Yep. Had to. We got to eat, you know."

"Eat?" The word was a croak torn out of her throat. She sat down on the step and peered up at the man/boy. "Eat?"

"Yep. Course, after I had me a steak or two, I was glad we had the meat. Ma said they're ain't nothin' better'n beef that you raised and butchered with your own two hands."

"Butchered." The word was small and strangled. "Butchered? Oh! Of course, butchered *beef!*"

"You okay, ma'am? You're lookin' a mite peaked."

"I'm fine, Stanley. Just fine. I had me a scare, but

give me a few minutes, and I'm sure my heart will start beating again."

"Huh?"

"Never mind." She smiled as she rose to her feet. "What do you say you and I start all over, back at the beginning? Tell me what's wrong with your . . . your cow."

"Already told you, ma'am. Milk's like water, 'n' she's swollen some. Red too. Ma's 'fraid she'll stop givin' if we don't get her well, and we depend on sellin' that milk for our cash money."

"Oh, Stanley," she muttered softly to herself, "if only you'd said so from the beginning." Meghan leaned against a porch post and turned away from Stanley's watchful eyes while her body shook with laughter, tears streaming down her face. "I thought . . . I thought . . . he'd killed . . ." And the laughter started again. After a few more minutes of being out of control, she took a hiccup of air and turned back to Stanley, who was patiently waiting for this strange woman to gather up her herbs and come help their cow.

"Stanley, I know just what to do for your cow."

"You do?" he answered doubtfully.

"Yep." She felt the laughter threatening again. "Yep, I do. If you'd like to sit here on this step, I'll hurry back inside and gather up my herbs. Then we'll be on our way to help your"—she chuckled—"your cow. Sound good?"

"Sounds like what I asked you fer, ma'am, right at the beginning."

"You're absolutely right, Stanley. Absolutely right."

Chapter Fourteen

Stanley took off with Meghan following. His feet were big and his legs long, and she had to half run to keep up.

"Stanley!" she called. "Stanley, could you slow down?"

"Sorry, ma'am, but Ma said not to play around."

"Believe me, Stanley," she said, gasping for breath, "we're not playing around."

"Huh?"

"Nothing," she called as he took off again.

If Stanley slowed his pace, Meghan didn't notice it any. She kept him in sight, losing him briefly when he went around a bend in the mountain trail. Finally she caught up with him waiting beside a slow-moving creek.

" 'Pears I'll have to carry you across, ma'am," he said, coming toward her.

"Carry me? No, I don't think so," she said, adamantly

holding up a hand. "I'm quite capable of crossing this small stream on my own power, Stanley."

"You're sure, ma'am? You're right puny-like. Don't want you fallin' in. Ma'd skin me alive if something happened to you 'fore our cow got fixed."

Meghan shook her head. "Well, you'll just have to take my word for it. I'm not puny." Meghan's lips twitched in silent laughter as she put on her best robust look.

"Them rocks is slick. You'll have to step real easy from one to another. See?" he said, taking off across the stream.

Meghan watched as one big foot after the other smacked the water, sending a spray of droplets high into the air.

He reached the other bank, then turned, waiting for her. "See, ma'am?" he repeated, his voice loud in the stillness of the valley, "You got to be real careful-like."

"I sure do, Stanley," she called as she stepped lightly from one rock to another, reaching the bank without a drop on her.

The hills gave way to a pasture bordering a small house and shed. The yard was neat and clean with a scattering of hens pecking at bugs. Several were busy making dust baths with a lot of clucking, scratching, and puffing of feathers before plopping belly-down in the hollow they'd made in the ground. Then, opening their wings wide, they fanned a "bath" of the dry dirt beneath them. Dust flew up into the air and, like rainfall, settled onto their backs. Bath complete, they would jump up, shake their fat bodies, and take off on a clumsy, neck-extended run to hunt for more bugs, or better yet, steal one away from another set of beady eyes.

The peaceful quiet was broken by the screech of "Stanley!" Onto the porch stepped the scrawniest woman Meghan had ever seen. Her legs looked like twigs stuffed into too-big shoes, and the rest of her was angular and rawboned. Her face was wrinkled and pinched, and her hair was drawn up on top of her head into a small gray knot. Meghan felt sure the pinched look on the woman's face was caused by the skintight hairdo.

"Well, boy!" she bellowed. "Took your time getting back." She scolded the boy without once acknowledging Meghan. Then she turned a set of piercing, dark-as-night eyes on Meghan. "Who you got there?" she asked her son.

"Why, Ma, you told me to get the herb woman. I brung her back, just like you said. We hurried some, but it took me some time to get her to knowed what I was needin'." His voice lowered in a conspiratorial tone, as if Meghan's ignorance was a secret between them.

"Don't you lie to me, boy. I know the herb lady, and that ain't her. You went and made a mistake, just when I was dependin' on you." Her accusatory voice cut the air like a knife.

Stanley hung his head, his entire body slumped.

"Excuse me," Meghan broke in, getting a baleful look from the woman. "Stanley didn't make a mistake. I am the herb woman." Meghan paused, wondering at how easily her tongue had wrapped around the identifying words of *herb woman*.

Well, I am, an herb woman, she thought, and she smiled to herself.

"You sayin' I'm lyin'?" The woman's chin jutted out, and Stanley moved a step or two away from Meghan, leaving her exposed and vulnerable.

"No, Mrs. Black—I assume you're Mrs. Black?" Meghan asked.

She got a short, affirmative nod for her answer.

"Yes, Mrs. Black," she went on, "as I said, I am the herb woman."

"And, as I said, you ain't." Her voice left no room for argument.

"I met the herb lady once, and unless you grew younger 'stead of older, there's no way you could be her. You didn't now, did you?" she asked nastily. The top-knot on her head bobbed as she pinned Meghan with a look of satisfaction.

"No, ma'am, I didn't, but my granny grew older, and she died a few years ago. She raised me and taught me how to heal with herbs. I don't have all her knowledge or experience, but I believe I have enough to be of help. No one could have the knowledge about healing that Granny had."

"Well, 'pears as if she taught you respect for your elders anyway. You say you know what you're doin'?

"Yes, ma'am, I do. I also believe I know what's wrong with your milk cow," Meghan said. "Stanley did an excellent job of explaining the problem."

He stood to one side, scuffing a foot in the dry dirt, eyes down as if the dust flying around his shoe was of paramount importance. Suddenly his head flew up, a wide smile on his face. "I did?"

"He did?" Mrs. Black asked, her voice as narrow as her eyes.

"He did," Meghan affirmed. "And, as Stanley said, I was the one that had trouble knowin' what he was needin'. I mean . . ." She almost chuckled, thinking that the situation would only go from bad to worse once she started talking like Stanley. "What he needed."

"Hmmpf." The all-knowing grunt was Mrs. Black's only reply.

"If you would be so good as to let me look at your cow, I'll sure do my best to make her better. Of course, I need to tell you I've never doctored a cow, and I'm not sure my herbs will have the same healing effects on an animal as on a human." She added, musing, "But I don't know why they wouldn't." She was rewarded for her honesty by another "Hmmpf."

Silence stretched between them as Meghan endured another piercing look.

Mrs. Black took a deep breath. She pursed her lips, then wiggled her mouth back and forth as she wrestled with the decision of whether to trust this girl with her cow or not.

"Well," she said, "it don't 'pear as if I have much of a choice. You're all I got." She gave Meghan a disparaging look. "Come on," she said, moving past Meghan, her bony legs pumping in tight, nervous steps.

"Thank you," Meghan said. "I think." She hurried after the woman. Stanley followed close behind, to a fenced barnyard where a Jersey cow stood chewing her cud, balefully watching the trio approach.

Mrs. Black stuck out her pigeon chest with pride. The cow obviously met with more approval than Meghan or Stanley.

Meghan felt she had to say something to fill the pregnant silence. "She . . . she's pretty?" Meghan raised her eyebrows in question, hoping her comment met Mrs. Black's expectations.

"She certainly is," Mrs. Black boomed. "She's a beauty. Name's Summer. Well, don't just stand there. Look her over." She pointed to the cow's udder.

Meghan slowly approached, stopping short when Summer swung her head and gave her horns a shake. Meghan shrank back.

"You watch those horns now, you hear? She could hook you good."

"Will she want to?" Meghan asked, her voice small.

"Course not, unless you make her mad."

"Uh, Mrs. Black, I'm a little . . . I'm not sure," Meghan stammered weakly. "What makes her mad?"

"You gonna look her over or not?" It was apparent Mrs. Black's limited patience was giving out.

"Yes. Yes," Meghan said more forcefully, "I am." Gulping, she took a few more steps toward Summer, then tentatively reached out and laid a nervous hand on the cow's rump. Other than blinking her big brown eyes a few times, Summer deigned not to acknowledge the touch. Her hide was warm from the autumn sun, and a grassy, milky smell emanated from the placid beast.

"Them ain't the two." Stanley's voice pierced the apprehensive quiet.

Meghan jumped. "What?"

"I said, them ain't the two." A long finger pointed. "It's the two on the other side, near Ma."

"Oh," Meghan said, feeling unqualified for the job at hand as she circled the cow, giving the back end wide berth. She kept one eye on Summer's horns and ran her palm over the udder. The cow's skin rippled, but that was the only sign it gave of the contact. The udder felt swollen and warm to Meghan. And while she'd never had any experience with cows, she had treated nursing mothers with similar symptoms. She wracked her brain, trying to remember anything she'd read about cows and their ailments. There was something called mastitis, where the udder got infected and swollen. However, mastitis was said to be caused by filth or manure entering the milk ducts. She glanced at the clean, neat barnyard. There was no obvious filth or excess manure in sight.

She glanced toward the barn. "Is that where you milk?"

"Yep," Stanley answered. "I do the milkin'. I'm in charge. Wanna see it?"

"Yes," Meghan answered with a smile. "I would."

She backed away from the cow and followed Stanley into the dark recess of the barn. A warm, musty, not unpleasant smell greeted her. She stood still, blinking as her eyes adjusted to the darkness. When she was able to see, it became immediately apparent that the barn would in no way classify as dirty. Fresh straw was scattered over a hard-packed dirtfloor.

"This is it," Stanley said, his chest stuck out. "This is where I milk." He beamed, as proud of his milking arena as a physician would be of his operating room. He was king of this domain as he stood with arms spread out over what looked to be a wooden gate.

"This here's a stanchion," he said proudly, his tongue curling around the word.

"A stanchion?"

"Yep."

Mrs. Black's voice boomed from behind, startling Meghan. "It's for milkin'. You stick the cow's head in there and lock her in. She can't move."

"Oh," Meghan said in a small voice, and she stopped closer for a better look.

"See?" Stanley said, opening the gate. "This here hole's for her head. Then, when she puts it in there, you shut it." And shut it he did. The two pieces of wood banged together with a vengeance. "It holds right steady while you milk." He was all smiles. "Next I put some grain in the pan, and she gets to eatin' and forgets all about being locked in. Say, wanna put your head in there? I can show you real easy-like how it works."

Meghan stepped back so there would be no misunderstanding that she most definitely did not want to put her head in there. At her refusal, Stanley eagerly stepped forward and stuck *his* head into the hole. He rotated his neck he could look up at her with a big grin. "See?

Works real good. If you want to lock it, go ahead. I won't mind none. I've done it afore myself, but it's kinda hard to get it back open without bein' able to see what you're doin. Go ahead," he urged, excited at the prospect of playing such an important role in her education.

"Stanley, you get yourself outta there and stop actin' like a fool. She can see without your big head stuck in where it shouldn't be. Now get out." Mrs. Black's voice cut like a whip, and he jumped back, bumping his head in the process, his face red.

"Thank you, Stanley." Meghan felt instant compassion for the embarrassed young man. "That demonstration really helped me see how it worked." She gave the feisty, outspoken woman a look.

Mrs. Black was not at all cowed. "Well?" she asked impatiently.

"Mrs. Black, I'm fairly certain Summer's, uh, milking apparatus," she faltered, uncertain of the polite word to use, "is caked up. Two of them, that is." She smiled toward Stanley, acknowledging his earlier pointing out of which two were the problem. "This can happen when cows are in a dirty environment and get manure on their bag, causing a type of infection. I'm fairly certain that's what happened to Summer, but your barn is certainly clean, so I'm not sure how it happened."

"Course it's clean," Mrs. Black said belligerently. "Well, don't matter none how it happened. Question is, can you fix it or not?" Mrs. Black cut to the heart of the matter.

"Uh, Ma, Summer likes manure." Stanley's words hung suspended like a gulp of indrawn air. "Remember? I told you."

"What?" Mrs. Black stepped back and pierced him with a look that would cause a strong man to shrink. "What do you mean she likes manure, and, no, I don't remember. Sometimes I wonder about you, Stanley. I surely do. I swear."

"Ain't makin' it up, Ma. Summer likes to lay on manure."

"What?" The one word sounded like the caw of a crow.

"Well, you see," he stumbled, "there's that pile of the manure we haul out from the barnyard, in the lower pasture?" He paused, waiting for acknowledgment. None coming, he plowed on. "She sure does enjoy headin' out that way and ploppin' herself down on it while she chews her cud. It's in the sun, and Summer really likes it on a cold day. It's smelly, but she don't mind that none. I recollect as to how she does this every chance she gets, 'cause there's always dried manure on her bag. I brush it off good, though, before milking. I know you're particular, Ma." His voice got quieter as his story wound down and his ma gave no evidence of understanding or condoning her cow's apparent delight in the manure pile, warm or not.

Meghan waited for some response to this tale of Summer's transgression. When it become apparent none was forthcoming, she ventured a response. "Well. Isn't it good we know how it happened?" She smiled hopefully at the frowning woman.

"Hmmpf."

Meghan gulped. "Well, now that the mystery's solved, let's see if what I'm prepared to try helps."

"'Bout time, young lady. Hope you're quicker at your healing than you've shown so far." She crossed her arms and glared at Meghan, daring any response.

Meghan closed her eyes, summing up all the patience she had. Mrs. Black was providing an experience she wouldn't soon forget. Poor Stanley.

"Stanley, first of all Summer must be kept very clean."

"Yes, ma'am. Like I said, I brush her off real good before milkin'."

"I'm sure you do, but we'll have to go one step further. You'll have to get a bucket of very warm water and hold a compress to her bag several times a day." She glanced up at the look of total bewilderment on Stanley's homely face.

"Uh, I'm not doing a very good job of explaining things, am I?" The question was asked of no one in particular, but Stanley did his best to answer.

"No, ma'am. You sure ain't."

"Yes, well, I'll try harder. Take Summer to the barn where you milk. Put her head in the stanchion to help hold her still. Carry a bucket of very warm water with you. Dip a clean rag in to the bucket of *very warm water,*" she said, emphasizing the last few words, "wring it out, then hold it against Summer's bag until the rag cools. When it cools, dip it in the warm water again, wring it out again, and hold it against her again. Keep doing that for several minutes, four or five times a day."

She gave the instructions in short, concise sentences to help him remember.

Her reward was great. Stanley's head was bobbing up and down, and a smile creased his face.

"But that's not all."

"It ain't?" Stanley asked apprehensively. He knew he could handle everything Meghan had said so far, but he wasn't sure about anything else.

Meghan gave a conspiratorial wink to Stanley. "I'll need your help, Mrs. Black." She had to swallow a grin at the look on the stern woman's face. "I'd like to make a potato-ginger poultice. If you could furnish me with a medium-size white potato and a grater, I'll grate the potato, then add fresh ginger root. When it's mixed, I'll put some into a clean rag and, Stanley, here's where we'll need your excellent help again. You'll need to hold the poultice against Summer's bag until the mixture becomes warm. Then you'll remove it, throw the used portion away, put some more into the rag, and apply it again. You can do this a couple of times a day. When you've completed this treatment, dry her bag, and apply some of this ointment I've made out of calendula. It'll keep her skin from cracking and help her heal. I'll mix up enough poultice to last a week."

She turned back to the woman. "Mrs. Black, if she isn't better in a few days, don't wait. Come get me, and we'll try something else, but I think this will do it. And, of course, no more manure pile for Summer."

Meghan took a deep breath. If she was looking for verbal approval or encouragement from Mrs. Black, she wasn't going to get it. However, she sensed respect in the way the woman looked at her, raised eyebrows and all.

"Well, don't just stand there, come along. Guess you'll be needin' my kitchen for your concoction. Stanley," she barked, "grab us a couple of those spuds outta the potato cellar. Potatoes on a cow. If that don't beat all. Yessiree, if that don't beat all."

Chapter Fifteen

Meghan felt as if it were raining inside of her as well as outside. The day was dark and dreary, and so was she. It had been a week since Conner left for what was to have been only a few days. She reminded herself that he didn't owe her any explanation or have any obligation to even let her know when he returned. She also reminded herself that, up until a few weeks ago, Conner Hendrickson hadn't even existed in her life.

She turned away from the window, only to have her rainy-day musings interrupted by a knock on the door, followed by a holler of, "Miss Meghan, you home?"

"Stanley?" She opened the door, and, sure enough, there he stood, rain dripping off the end of an old slouch hat. "Come in. You're drenched. Is Summer worse? Is that why you're out on a day like this?" She stepped back, giving him room to drip on the rag rug in front of the door.

"No, ma'am. She ain't worse."

"Do you need something else?"

"No, ma'am. Don't need anythin'."

Meghan started to ask another question, then remembered that this was Stanley, and Stanley had his own way of getting to the point. Questioning would only sidetrack him, and then the outcome would be anyone's guess.

She motioned him to a chair and was about to ask him if he'd like to take off his wet jacket when she noticed the bleached flour sack he held tightly in one hand. It moved.

Stanley raised it until it was even with his nose. "Hey, there," he said to the sack, "you just hold your horses. I ain't ready for you yet, and you're spoiling the surprise."

Meghan waited. He was like a horse when it got a bit between its teeth; he'd take off on his own at any moment. She looked warily at the sack, hoping Stanley had a tight hold, keeping inside whatever was doing the moving.

"Summer's fine," he volunteered at last. "Ma's real pleased. She says we're goin' through potatoes like a rootin' hog." He took a breath of air, then gingerly set the sack on the floor between his big feet. He carefully opened it enough for one big hand to fish inside. Meghan stepped back. He grabbed something and slowly pulled it out.

"Here," he said, and he shoved a folded quilt toward

her. "Ma made it herself," he said proudly. "It's called a log cabin. She drew the pattern and picked out all the pieces. I helped some. I cut some of the pieces so's she could sew 'em."

"Oh, Stanley," Meghan breathed, "it's absolutely beautiful. You said your mother made it?"

"Yep."

Meghan opened up the quilt and laid it reverently on the kitchen table. The log-cabin design stood out vivid in colors. It was art in its purest form. She stood over it, admiring the colors, running a hand over each evenly placed tiny stitch. It must have taken hours and hours of painstaking work.

"Oh, Stanley, thank you, but I can't accept it."

"Huh?" Stanley straightened up, one hand still holding the sack closed. "You can't? Why not, Miss Meghan?"

"It's too beautiful. Too much. This is an heirloom." She glanced up at him, his face showing his lack of understanding of not only her refusal but her last word.

"Don't know what one of them is, but I can tell you Ma'd be real mad if you didn't want her quilt. Oh, dang it, I forgot to tell you what Ma said I was supposed to say when I gave it to you."

He screwed up his face in concentration. "Ma said: 'Thank you. The poultice is workin' real good. Summer is well.'" He stopped, his eyes still closed in concentration. Then a smile broke out on his face. "She said: 'I want you to have this quilt. It's to pay you for makin' Summer better. And would you please send back with Stanley'"—he grinned at her—"that's me—Somethin' for the pain in my hands. They hurt some, and on rainy days they get stiff.' Whew! I remembered everything."

Meghan gently began folding the quilt. "I'd be proud to accept this, then. Please tell your mother it will go on my bed right now, and I'll look at it every day with pleasure. Can you do that, Stanley?"

He nodded his head. "Yep. That's a lot littler than what Ma made me tell you." Then he made a face. "Doggone it, I done went and almost forgot." He held up the sack. "I brung you a present too." He opened the sack and started fishing around inside it.

Meghan held her breath. "That's okay, Stanley, you didn't have to." But before she could finish, Stanley pulled his gift out. The empty sack fell to his feet. A tiny *mew* emitted from within the cup of his hands.

Another *mew* split the air, stronger this time and filled with outrage. Being transported in a sack certainly wasn't acceptable.

"A kitten. How sweet." Meghan was all smiles as she stepped forward and took the mewing creature from Stanley. It was completely white with a tiny pink nose. One eye was shut, but the other peered intently at Meghan. Then it gave another cry, this one louder and more plaintive.

"It's probably hungry," Stanley volunteered. "Our barn cat had a whole bunch, and this one's the littlest of 'em all. The others pushed it away when it went to nurse. I tried to help, but when I wasn't there, I don't think she got to eat at all. Her one eye's kinda bad. The mother cat didn't keep her as clean as she did the rest of 'em. Ain't she pretty?" The words poured out of Stanley while he watched and waited for Meghan's agreement.

"She's beautiful. I don't think there's a drop of any other color but white on her. Oh, Stanley, this is a wonderful gift." She snuggled the kitten to her face, feeling the small heart beat in her hands. "I'm going to call her Snow. What do you think?"

It was impossible for Stanley to beam more. "Snow's a right pretty name, Miss Meghan. Fits her fine. You really like her?"

"I love her." Meghan laughed as the kitten's rough tongue licked her finger.

"She's white like snow, all right." He laid one big finger on the kitten's small head, his touch gentle.

"If you'll hold her a moment," she said, placing the kitten in his big hand, "I'll get her some milk. We'll take care of that empty belly right now, Snow," she crooned to the kitten. Meghan moved toward the door. "It's in the root cellar. I'll be right back."

She reached for the door latch, then jumped back, startled, as a knock sounded through the wooden frame.

Her hand faltered, and then she opened the door. Waves of delight swept over her.

"Conner." She breathed his name. "Oh, Conner, I'm so glad to see you." The words tumbled out unchecked as joy overwhelmed her. He smiled down at her, pleasure in his eyes at her unrestrained welcome. Meghan closed her eyes. The man standing in front of her was so very handsome as he blocked out the rain and drear.

It was as if the sun had broken through, and he was the rainbow in the darkened sky.

He reached toward her, pulling her into his arms. Putting his face into her hair, he inhaled its fresh summer scent. Then he tilted her face toward him and whispered her name. "Meghan, my Meghan." Before he could say more, he noticed the tall boy standing in the shadows of the room. He stepped back and raised a quizzical eyebrow at Meghan.

"Stanley?" She cleared her too-dry throat. "Come here. I'd like you to meet Conner Hendrickson. Stanley just brought me gifts from him and his mother."

Conner released her, leaving her already missing his touch. He smiled and held out a hand to Stanley. "Stanley, how are you?"

"Fine, Mr Hendrickson." He shifted the kitten to his other hand while he vigorously pumped Conner's outstretched one.

"How's your mother?"

"Ma's fine."

"And Summer?"

Meghan broke in, surprise written on her face. "You two already know each other?"

"You bet we do," Conner answered for both of them. "Stanley and Mrs. Black furnish Bonnie her milk. Of course, Summer helps, right, Stanley?"

Stanley chuckled. "You bet. But Summer got real sick, Mr. Hendrickson. An' Miss Meghan healed her. You know why?"

"No, I don't." His eyes danced as he waited for Stanley's answer.

"'Cause she's the herb lady," he said, proud of his ability to roll out the strange-sounding word. "She's real smart."

Conner's voice was soft as he looked at Meghan, her eyes wide in her lovely face. "Yes, she is, Stanley. She healed Bonnie, and now"—he paused—"now she's working on healing me."

"You sick, Mr. Hendrickson?" Concern laced Stanley's question.

"You might say that, Stanley. Not sick like, uh sick"—he fumbled for words—"but, uh, needing healing like . . . help me out here, Meghan."

A smile hovered on her full lips. "You're doing just fine, Conner. Your feet almost fit, both of them."

Stanley looked from one to the other. Neither one of the adults was making any sense at all. But then, adults rarely did make sense, the way he saw it. Then his eyes widened with remembering. "Oh, no. I've been here too long. Ma'll be mad. She said . . ."

"Not to play around." Meghan's voice joined his as she parodied his mother's dire warning. "I understand, Stanley. I'll get something for your mother's hands." She went to a cupboard in the kitchen, feeling the eyes of both males follow her. She quickly returned with two containers.

"Stanley, these herbs need to be made up in a tea." She held up one of the containers. "Have your mother drink this throughout the day. "It's made up of black cohosh and blessed thistle as well as burdock. The burdock is an excellent blood purifier. It will help reduce swelling in her joints so she'll feel relief during the damp weather when her hands are stiff and aching."

She looked up at the totally bewildered boy. "It's okay, Stanley. You don't have to remember all that." She smiled at him. "All you have to remember is that the herbs in this container are to be made up into a tea. And this . . ." She held up a smaller tin. "This is a salve made up of several herbs such as comfrey that will help reduce any inflammation or swelling. She can rub this into her hands anytime she feels the need."

Stanley traded the white kitten for the two tins and dropped them into the now empty flour sack. Nodding his head at all Meghan had told him, he pulled his hat tighter onto his head and, squaring his shoulders, opened the door to the cold drizzle.

"Stanley, you be careful. Tell your mother I said hello and that I'll be stopping by for Bonnie's milk now that we're back." Conner gave the boy a pat on the back.

"I sure will, Mr. Hendrickson. And, Miss Meghan, I'm awfully glad you like Snow. I'll be comin' back to see her. Bet she'll fatten right up. I'll give Ma the herbs." And with that he stepped out into the rain.

Meghan slowly closed the door, then turned back to the cheery room and the man who had made it so.

Chapter Sixteen

Meghan smiled at Conner, suddenly shy. The Conner who'd greeted her was different from the man who had told her good-bye. She glanced down at the kitten in her hands and was glad for the distraction. Then she offered snow to Conner.

"Would you mind babysitting for a few minutes while I go out to the root cellar and get some milk for this hungry one?" She thrust the kitten into his hands, not giving him time to respond. She hurried out the door. The walkway between the cabin and the root cellar was covered with a wooden roof. Granny had made it that way so they could come and go between the two structures without too much exposure to the elements.

She pushed open the root cellar door, glad that the errand gave her a few moments to regain her composure, regretful that it had taken her out of Conner's presence.

The root cellar had an odor all its own, a pleasant blend of apples, carrots, onions, potatoes, hay, and dirt. The air was cool, the dirt dry. In a dark corner Granny had created a storage chamber out of bales of hay. The hay bales lay in a rectangle with an opening in the center. The opening was lined with straw. Additional bales of hay acted as a lid for the opening. Meghan pushed one of the "lids" aside and reached down, brushing straw off the wooden top of a small crock. She placed the crock of milk on the ground and carefully rearranged the straw back over the remaining crocks. Then she put the hay lid back over the hole and, carefully shutting the root cellar door, hurried back to the cabin.

"I think you'd better hurry," Conner said, his smile wide. "This one's mighty hungry."

"Oh, poor baby." Meghan gave the kitten a pat as she poured some milk into a saucer. She took the kitten out of Conner's hand and put it in front of the milk. The kitten sniffed at it, sneezed and took two quick steps backward. Meghan laughed as it tried to shake a drop of milk off a small whisker.

"Here, let me." Conner picked the kitten up, then dipped a finger into the milk and quickly transferred it to the kitten's mouth. The kitten tried to turn away from Conner's wet touch, but he was persistent. He dipped his finger again and again. The last time a tiny pink tongue darted forward and tentatively licked at the drop. That was all it took. Conner gently placed her again in front of the bowl, but this time there was no backing up. She put her mouth to the bowl and, with pink tongue darting back and forth, began lapping up the milk. The only lull in her drinking was when, in her exuberance, milk got up her nose, and she gave several small sneezes.

By this time both Conner and Meghan were on their knees cheering the small animal on, delighting in its antics.

"You know," Conner said, rising and holding his hand out to Meghan, "I'm getting worried about you."

"You are?" she asked, perplexed, putting her hand in his, letting him help her up. "Why on earth would you be worried about me?"

"Because every time I turn my back, you've got another mouth to feed."

"You're right." She laughed. "My family is increasing by leaps and bounds. You should see Scrapper. He's getting so fat, he waddles."

He reluctantly released her hand, then reached into his pocket. "It also seems like it's your day for getting presents too."

She held still.

"A present? Why on earth would you give me a present? It's not Christmas," she said, trying for a lightness she was far from feeling. "And it's not my birthday."

"No, it's not, but I missed your birthday, and I missed Christmas."

"Conner, you didn't even know me on my birthday or Christmas." She shook her head in mock exasperation, loving the way his smile brought out the dimples at the sides of his mouth.

"Doesn't matter. I know you now. And this gift is for

all the Christmases and birthdays I've missed. Sit down Meghan. Please."

She didn't move for a moment, then, bending over and picking up a replete Snow, she walked to the rocking chair and sat down. Feeling somewhat foolish, she said, "Okay, Mr. Hendrickson, I'm ready."

He stood watching her, loving the trusting yet apprehensive look on her face, loving the way her hair curled around her face as it fell to her shoulders. Loving the woman he'd fought all week against loving until, in exasperation, he'd given in and acknowledged his feelings. He'd given in and allowed the seeds of trust and hope to germinate and grow. And once he'd given in, he'd been filled with a sense of rightness. And from that moment on he'd acted with a sense of purpose that he'd thought he'd never possess again.

He held out a small box that looked a bit worn. Placing it in her palm, he said, "This was my grandmother's. I took it out of a safe box I keep in the bank in Helena, and I want you to have it." Sensing her pull back in refusal, he went on, "Please, Meghan." He put his large hand over her smaller one and gently closed her fingers around the box. "Do you remember the day I left, I told you I needed time and that maybe . . ."

"Yes." Her one word was weak and quiet.

"And," he said, smiling, "I also said there was something I wanted to share with you?"

"Yes."

"And you were curious—very curious, if I remember right."

"Conner," she said warningly.

"Are you still curious?" He asked, delighting in tantalizing her.

"Conner, you are—"

"Now just be patient. I'm about to satisfy that curiosity. Now, let's see, where was I?" He paused, a devilish look on his face.

"Mister, you are enjoying this way too much." She pursed her lips and shook her head at him. "Now, what if I don't think there's something you should share with me?" She tilted her head, looking at him with a half smile.

"Then you'd be wrong."

"Oh, I would, would I?" Her hand enclosed the small box, and it felt as if the contents were burning through to her heart.

"Yes, you would. But before I tell you, why don't you open your present? You're about to crush the box."

"You, Conner Hendrickson, are incorrigible."

The words hung in the air, ineffective and meaningless, as she gently took the lid off the box, removed a small piece of cotton, then froze, breath held as she looked at the contents nestled on a cotton bed. With trembling fingers she reached in and lifted out an oval brooch. The rim of the pin was gold filigree edging as delicate as the finest lace. But the middle was what caught Meghan's eye, for it seemed to reach out and catch all the light. In a nest of small sapphire chips rested a large cobalt blue sapphire. Each facet of the stone caught and bent the light, then reflected it back in a multitude of blues. Each variation of blue, be it the deep, almost black center of the stone to the brilliant blues of the edge, was ever-changing and breathtaking. It was exquisite.

She raised her eyes from the jewel to search Conner's face. He was looking fully at her, watching her, waiting for her reaction, hoping for her approval and acceptance.

"Don't you like it?" His question was hushed and fearful.

"Oh, Conner. It's breathtaking. I love it." She turned it in her hand, watching again the play of light. Then, in a quiet voice, she said, "But I can't accept it. It's worth a fortune, and . . . and . . ." Words momentarily failed her as she looked up at him with unshed tears in her eyes. "It belongs in your family. Your grandmother would want Bonnie or your wife to have it, not a stranger." Resolutely she shut away its brilliance as she laid it back in the box. Her heart was heavy.

"Meghan." With gentle fingers, he raised her face to his. "What I want to share with you is . . . is me. No." He held her face firm, making her look at him, not letting her turn away from what he needed to say. "Because you are what's lacking my life, and I from yours. I guessed it the day I left. But I never realized just how much you have invaded my life and my dreams in such a short period of time. In Helena I had the time I needed to listen to my heart and to acknowledge my feelings. I'm not afraid anymore. Meghan, I want you to be my—"

"Stop." She pressed two fingers against his lips, refusing to let him complete the sentence. "Don't say it,

Conner. Don't ask it, please. I can't be any more to you than what I am now—a friend."

He took a step back, his eyes dark with hurt.

"Don't you see? You and I are from different lifestyles. Very different lifestyles. You're accustomed to wealth and all that goes with it. I'm not. Look around you, Conner." She spread her hands to take in the small cabin. "This is what I am. I'm Meghan O'Reiley, orphan, taken in, raised, and loved by a dear, sweet woman. I wouldn't know what to do, or how to act. I've never entertained, and I've never been entertained in the style you're accustomed to. My idea of a dinner party is having a close friend over for a very simple meal." She smiled at him. "Like your stew. My experience of a home is this: my small cabin. You're lived on a much grander scale. I wouldn't know what to do in your life. Miss Fairchild's prepared me somewhat, but . . ."

She stopped, tears rolling down her face, pain in her heart at what she knew she had to do, what she had to say.

"Oh, Meghan." His voice was hoarse with emotion, "You're wrong, so wrong. We're not that different. We're not rivers apart. I know you feel something for me. I see it in your eyes. I know it by your tears. You don't shed tears for someone or something you don't care about. I've rushed you. I've moved too quickly. I've had days to think, while you haven't had time to even contemplate sharing your life with Bonnie and me. Please keep the pin as a gift from one friend, one very special friend, to another. My grandmother would like that, and so would I. And friends we'll be, at least for now. At least until I'm able to lay all your fears to rest and show you that you would fit into my life, because, you see, you've already fit into my heart. I'm going to leave now." He slowly walked toward the door. "But"—he turned, a smile on his mouth if not in his eyes—"I'll be back. You owe me a supper, Meghan O'Reiley, and I expect you to keep your promise."

He walked out into the rainy day, shutting the door behind him, leaving her holding his gift and his heart in her hand.

Chapter Seventeen

'*D*ear Son,' the letter read, *I hope this letter will get to you before we arrive. Your mother and I have decided that since you won't bring that precious baby to meet her grandparents, her grandparents will have to come to her. I've got some mine business that could use my personal attention, so we'll be combining business with pleasure. We should arrive in Helena in two weeks. Don't worry about meeting us there. Your mother won't want to wait, so we'll hire a rig and come directly to Pig Eye Gulch. Don't go to a lot of trouble. Your cabin will be just fine. Father.*

Conner lowered the letter and sighed. He loved his parents, and he would enjoy seeing them and showing off Bonnie. But there was a part of him that dreaded the visit. First of all, there had been angry words between him and his. Was all forgiven? And his cabin would not

172

be "just fine." It was one room. A large room, but certainly not the accommodations his parents were used to.

He ran a hand through his hair, then threw the letter onto the table. There had to be a positive side to this visit; he just had to find it.

"Bonnie," he said to the little girl sitting on a rug playing with her doll and horse, "we need help. And"—he smiled, picking her up and holding her above his head, shaking giggles out of her—"I know just where to get it. Would you be available, Miss Bonnie, to join your father in a walk?" The baby squealed and grabbed his hair with both fists.

"Ow. I'll take that as a yes." He laughed. He pried her fists loose, then set her back on the floor while he put on her coat and hat.

Meghan saw them before they got to her cabin. She was putting her garden to bed for the winter when she heard Lady gave a loud bark. As she looked up, her heart leaped, and a smile creased her face. Conner covered the ground in long strides. Bonnie hitched a ride on his wide shoulders.

Dropping the hoe to the ground, Meghan ran to the top of the path and waved. She hadn't seen Conner since that rainy day when he'd given her his gift. Every day since she'd promised herself she'd contact him and offer the invitation to supper, and every day she'd found a reason to put it off. Not that she didn't want to see him, she did, badly.

Now that he was here, she wondered why she had denied herself the pleasure of his company. Just seeing his smiling face, the corners of his eyes creased with pleasure, filled her with warmth and peacefulness. She knew she loved this man and his little girl.

Laughing and reaching for a smiling Bonnie, she was grateful that he had made the first move.

He swung Bonnie off his shoulders and into Meghan's waiting arms. His eyes swept over her, and he realized all over again how much he loved this delightful woman. Damp ringlets around her temples showed she'd been working. And there were two small freckles across the bridge of her nose.

"Come here, you little pixie. What are you doing in my neck of the woods, huh?" Meghan nuzzled the baby's neck reveling in the wet kisses and happy pats she got in return.

"We've come for advice and maybe a cup of coffee." Conner met her eyes.

"I'm glad you came, Conner. I was going to invite you to supper, but . . ."

"I know," he said, his voice full of understanding. "It's okay."

They walked shoulder to shoulder to the cabin, a quiet acceptance between them.

She took a deep breath, "Conner, would you like to come to supper?"

"Yes, ma'am, I surely would," he teased. "When?"

"Right now?" She raised her eyebrows in question. "Tonight?"

"Why, I believe I can, but I'd better check with the young lady squirming in your arms. Miss Bonnie, would you be interested in eating your supper at this lovely lady's table?" He paused, looking at Bonnie, then nodded. "The young lady says she would be delighted to eat mashed potatoes and gravy with you. She might even eat her vegetables without throwing or spitting them." He lowered his voice. "She's especially partial to peas. They're so easy to spit. Much better than carrots."

Meghan laughed, her fears and concerns instantly vanishing.

"Well, you are a lucky man, Conner Hendrickson. I just happen to have a roast and potatoes in the oven. Sorry, no peas, Bonnie, but I've heard," she said in a whisper, "that beets make a lovely mess when smeared on someone, such as a big, strong, father. They're a very pretty color."

"Hey, no fair." He held his hands up in supplication. "I'm one against two here."

The homey smell of something cooking greeted them as they went inside. Conner couldn't help but compare this cabin to his often lonely one.

Meghan spread a quilt on the floor and set Bonnie on it. Then she picked Snow up from the rocking chair.

"Look, Bonnie," Meghan said, "this is Snow." Bonnie gave a glad cry and reached for the kitten, but Meghan held it securely in her hands, knowing that Bonnie was too little to use caution with the small animal.

Looking over her shoulder, she said, "Conner, why don't you show Bonnie Snow while I get us a cup of coffee?"

"I'll get the coffee. You enjoy Bonnie. Say, didn't I

hear Lady barking when I came up the path? Where is she?"

"She's still wary of anyone else but me and, of course, Jeremy. She and that fat son of hers are still residing in my woodshed, but I suspect I'll have to make room for them in the house when winter arrives in full force. Not that I'll mind, but I'm not so sure about Snow. I introduced them the other day, and between arching her back and hissing, I don't think she made them feel too welcome in her domain." She turned back to the baby. "The cups are in the cupboard just over the sink."

Conner took two cups out of the cupboard and filled them both from the pot on the back of the stove. Taking them to the table, he glanced into the small sitting room. Meghan was opening a basket and taking out balls of yarn, spools, and wooden blocks. She put the arrangement of toys in front of Bonnie. Snow came over to investigate and gave a playful swat to one of the yarn balls. Bonnie leaned forward, jabbering and laughing at the kitten. She was totally enthralled with this new playmate and with the new toys in front of her.

Meghan joined Conner at the kitchen table. "I think Bonnie's entertained for a while, don't you?"

Conner chuckled. "I do, but I don't think Snow will be entertained if Bonnie gets those chubby hands around her and pulls her fur."

"I'm not worried. Snow's fast. Look, she's staying just out of reach."

"Mmm," Conner said, sipping his coffee. "Good coffee, good company."

"I agree. However, I do have something that would make this good coffee and good company even better."

"What?" he asked skeptically, a half smile on his face. "What could be better?"

"These." Meghan reached into a cupboard and pulled down a tin. Taking the lid off, she took out several cookies.

"Oatmeal?" Conner asked hopefully. "Maybe oatmeal raisin?"

"Oatmeal raisin it is. I don't suppose you want one," she teased.

"No, I don't."

"You don't?" The smile on her face was replaced by a look of surprise.

"Nope. I don't want one. I want two, three, maybe even four."

"Oh, you! You had me worried for a moment." She put the plate in front of him. "Do you mind if Bonnie tries half of one? She and her father might ruin their supper if they eat too many," she scolded. "However, she'll probably make a mess."

"Now, do you think I could sit here and eat these without giving her any? And, you're right, she will make a mess, but she'll wash. So will her clothes. Believe me, I know they'll wash. It seems that all I do is wash for Miss Bonnie. My hands are getting red and raw." He laughed and held out his hands for her to inspect.

She looked them over. "Not one bit of redness, and they certainly aren't raw. I'm beginning to believe you delight in spinning tales, Conner."

"No, not usually. But you, my Meghan"—his voice lowered—"are so very easy to tease."

They looked at each other, then both took a sip of coffee, trying to act as if drinking coffee was all they had on their minds.

Meghan broke the silence. "You said you came for advice. I'm ready to try, but I need to warn you, I'm not that wise or worldly. My advice may not be worth anything at all."

"I guess, more than advice, I need to share a problem with a friend."

"What's wrong, Conner?" She leaned toward him.

He handed her the letter.

Conner drank his coffee, and Meghan slowly read the letter, then lowered it to the table.

"Conner?" She reached over and laid her hand on his. "The only advice I can give you is probably not what you want to hear."

"Go ahead. I need to hear what you think."

"Well, I think you're awfully lucky to have your mother and father. Not only do you have them, but they love you enough to come all the way from England to see you. My advice would be to enjoy every minute of their visit. Spend time with your father, and lay to rest any unhappiness between you, and let your mother thoroughly spoil Bonnie. That's what grandmothers do."

"Ah, Meghan. If only everyone were as understanding as you. But, sweetheart, it's not that simple. I agree, I need to spend time with my father. I love him dearly, and the quarrel was hard on both of us. My mother is an angel. Bonnie will love her."

"Then, Conner, tell me, what is it that you're worried about? Maybe I'm wrong, but I sense you miss them."

"I admit, I have been missing them." He took a deep breath. "Okay, here's what's worrying me. Where do I put them? My father may say that my cabin will be fine, but it won't. It won't be fine at all. It's one room, Meghan. And that one room is smaller than my bedroom at home was."

"But it's such a nice cabin. It's much nicer than many have in this valley."

"I know all that, but . . . My mother's a good sport. She'll go along with anything."

"And your father?"

"Oh, he'll go along, but all the while he'll be pointing out to me how much better I could be living in England."

They both grew quiet, Conner trying to picture his parents crowded into his cabin and Meghan trying to think how she could sell him on a solution that was beginning to form in her mind.

"Meghan?"

"Conner?"

Both looked up and spoke at the same time.

"You first," Conner said.

"No, you."

The moment was theirs alone as the walls of the cabin shielded them from everything but their pleasure in each other's company.

"Okay," he said. "I just want you to know how nice it is to have you to talk to. I think back to the first time

I met you"—he flushed, remembering ordering her out of his cabin—"and I don't think I was all that nice when I came to get the 'herb lady' to help me with Bonnie." He grimaced.

Meghan had to laugh. "Well, you were pretty fierce. I was so mad at you, I couldn't see straight. Then later, when I saw you with Bonnie . . . well, let's just say I changed my first opinion. But, I agree, it is nice to have someone to share problems with. Makes them seem smaller and less scary. And, I have to say, I'm glad I've gotten to know the real Conner Hendrickson. He's much nicer than the angry one." Her eyes softened to a cornflower blue. She waited a moment, pondering how best to present her solution to him.

"Conner, I think I have a solution to your problem, but first I have to ask you a question."

"Anything. Go ahead."

"No, it's not that easy. Your answer must be totally honest, even if you think you will hurt my feelings. Agree?"

"I'll always be honest with you, Meghan. Ask. I'm curious." He reached for her hand, seeking to reassure her.

She took a deep breath. "Okay. Conner, do you think your mother could like me?"

His brow wrinkled in puzzlement. "Meghan, what kind of question is that? How could anyone not like you? Of course she will."

"No, that's not enough. Please, Conner. Think about your answer."

He leaned back in his chair. "Meghan, my mother has

always wanted a daughter. She would delight in one like you. I can truthfully tell you that she would find you interesting and someone she would enjoy spending time with. She would see you as the kind and loving woman you are." He smiled. "Does that answer your question?"

"Yes. Yes, I think it does. I know you must think it an odd question, but when I tell you my solution, you'll understand. Thank you for your honesty, and"—she lowered her voice—"thank you for finding me worthy of your fond feelings."

His eyes never left hers as he waited for her to continue.

"I have two bedrooms. Granted, they're small, but . . . well, I'd like to offer one of them to your mother and Bonnie. Your father and you could share your cabin. During the day, your mother could bring Bonnie back home or stay here, whatever she desired. I'm called out often during the day, and I have chores that keep me busy. I wouldn't be in your mother's way much." She rushed the words. "You can all eat here—that is, if you want to—uh—if you don't want to cook. Conner, I'm not doing such a good job of this, but I really think we could work something out. We've got not one but two homes to offer them. And while neither one is on the scale of yours in England, combined they could make the visit pleasant for both you and them. I would love having your mother and Bonnie here."

He shook his head. "What a wonderful woman you are, Meghan O'Reiley. Amazing and wonderful. You're willing to open your home to strangers. Why?"

"Because they're your family. Because you're my . . ." Her voice failed her as she searched for a word to describe what he was to her. A word that would say enough without giving away her true feelings.

"Your friend?" He supplied the inadequate word.

"Yes," she whispered. "My very, very special friend." She raised her eyes to him. "What do you think, Conner? We can make it work. We really can."

His voice was low when he finally answered. "I think I'm a very lucky man. I never thought I'd be this happy again, or this lucky to have someone like you in my life. And I think yes, yes, yes." He beamed at her. "It's a perfect solution. It's taking advantage of you, but I'm going to be selfish enough not to let that stop me from saying yes."

"Oh, Conner. Thank you."

"Don't thank me. I'm the one who should be saying thanks."

"This will be fun, I know it will. I'll have another woman in the house to talk to. I've missed Granny so much. And I'll have this special little girl to enjoy and"— she said wickedly—"to spoil."

"Good grief, by the time I get her back from the two of you, she'll be rotten."

"Mmm, but a good rotten. Now, right after supper you and I have a lot of planning to do. We've got company coming. Company from England."

Chapter Eighteen

Company from England. The words dominated their minds in the days that followed. Meghan cleaned her cabin, then recleaned it. Conner cleaned his, and while it wasn't as thorough a job as Meghan's, it was sufficient. Bonnie bounced happily between the two homes and made friends not only with a wary Snow but with the roly-poly Scrapper. Even Lady accepted the extra coming and goings and spent a great deal of her time wagging her tail in greeting. She had attached herself to Conner, forming a bond that surprised both of them. The minute she saw him approaching, she began barking and dancing in happy circles, tail high, her legs springs as she waited for him to bend down and ruffle the fur around her neck.

Meghan had lost track of the times she'd asked, "Conner, when do you think they'll be here?"

His answer was always the same, frustrated, "I don't know. It should be any time now."

She spent time with Bonnie, secretly trying to coach the little girl to say "Grandma." But so far, all she had succeeded in getting was *mmmmmm,* a toothy drool, and a big smile. Perfectly acceptable.

Meghan tried to keep herself busy as a way of ignoring the crawly feeling in the pit of her stomach each time she thought of actually meeting Conner's parents. What if Conner was wrong and neither his mother or father liked her? What if they labeled her a gold digger too?

She looked around her cabin, trying to see it through his parents' eyes. Every sign of aging and wear suddenly changed from homey and welcoming to humble.

When she tried to share some of those fears with Conner, he only smiled and said she was worrying too much; his parents would love her and appreciate her hospitality tremendously.

She had neglected her friends, only doing quick checks on Marybeth to see how she and the expected baby were coming along. She hadn't even spent much time with Jimmy and felt guilty about leaving when he fussed at seeing her go.

It was with delight that she answered a knock at her cabin door to see Emery standing there. "How far apart are they?" she asked.

"Far apart?" Emery answered with a puzzled frown.

"The labor pains," Meghan prompted him, surprised by Emery's slowness at such a crucial time.

The man laughed, "Oh, no. That's not why I'm here, Meghan."

Meghan expelled a sigh, then took a couple of calming breaths.

"I'm sorry, Emery. It's just that seeing you standing there alone and Marybeth so close to her time, I jumped to conclusions."

"Now it's me that has to say sorry. I didn't even think about how my comin' here would naturally make you think the baby was on its way." He smiled at her. "We're all eager to see this new one, but I don't think anyone's as eager as Marybeth. Her back hurts, and she's tired of lookin' like she does. Course"—he lowered his eyes—"I think she's beautiful."

"She is," Meghan said. "She's beautiful not only on the outside but on the inside as well. I'm fortunate to have her as a friend."

"There's where we differ, Meghan. We feel fortunate to have you as our friend. And"—he cleared his throat—"that's why I'm here today."

"Come in," she invited.

He followed her into the kitchen and sat down at the table. His hands were busy fidgeting and picking at the tablecloth, looking at it instead of her. "I'm not sure how to ask this of you, so I'll just jump right in." He looked up at Meghan and, seeing her affirmative nod, went on. "Would you look after Marybeth and the children should somethin' happen to me?" The words poured out of him like an unchecked river. "What I'm askin' is a lot—I know that. But I'm worried about, well, about being killed in the mine."

"Oh, Emery." She reached over to console him, his fear vibrant in the room.

"It's risky work at best. Hendrickson's mine is better run than most, but still there are problems. Like right now. We've got several hotheads on our shift, and, frankly, they worry me. They're takin' risks and laughin' off any of our suggestions or worries."

"Does Conner know?"

"No. And I'm goin' to ask you to keep this conversation between you and me. Please don't tell Mr. Hendrickson or"—he paused—"Marybeth. She's got enough on her mind right now, and she sure don't need to worry about me. No"—he held up a hand to stop Meghan's attempted protests—"just trust me on this, please. Could be I'm worryin' about nothin'. So far we more experienced miners have been able to keep things in check. Shoot, could be I'm just bein' an old fussbudget. I'd tell Mr. Hendrickson, but several of us have talked it over, and we've agreed there's no need yet. We'd like to handle this ourselves for the time being. Gets out of hand, then we'll all go to him. I'm just . . . Heck, you know. I'm bein' silly. Let's just forget I came here and even mentioned my worry." He rose to his feet, moving toward the door.

"Emery," she called. "The answer is yes."

He stopped and turned toward her, an expectant look on his face.

"Yes, absolutely yes, I'll look after Marybeth and the children. I'm honored you asked me, but I'll pray every day it will never be necessary. I'll leave it up to you whether or not to alert Conner. I do know he'd respond quickly and without bringing you or the other workers into it. Safety is so very important to him. But this will be our secret, since you insist."

"Thank you, Meghan. I know I'm bein' silly, but Marybeth and Jimmy, and of course the new babe, are more important to me than anything else. I'll sleep better knowin' I talked to you. Say," he said, anxious now to talk of something else, "Marybeth tells me Mr. Hendrickson's parents are due any day now for their visit. You must be getting mighty anxious."

"*Anxious* isn't the word." She laughed. "I'm scared to death."

"Well, you have nothin' to be scared of. They can't help but like you."

"Thank you, Emery. I'll remember you said that. Tell Marybeth I'll be by tomorrow, and, by golly, this time I'll take time for tea, a visit, and a hug from Jimmy."

"I'll tell her."

She went back into the cabin, pondering their conversation, determined to ignore the cold hand of fear between her shoulders. Emery would be fine. Of course he would.

It was late that afternoon, and she was just putting the final swirl of Granny's seven-minute icing on a white layer cake when she heard Lady and her "company's coming" bark. Meghan put the empty frosting bowl into the dishpan and, wiping her hands on a towel, went outside. Obviously this was going to be a day for visitors and interruptions.

She went outside, expecting to see someone from the valley, possibly needing her help. What she saw instead was a buggy, the horses driven by a man who looked familiar. As it drew closer, her stomach gave a lurch. It was Conner. And the passengers—well, they had to be his parents. She looked closely at the man sitting in the buggy, his intent gaze taking in the cabin and surrounding landscape. While his bearing was erect and somewhat forbidding, he was an older replica of a man she knew and cared for. He was tall with wide shoulders. But where Conner's hair was dark, his father's was edged with streaks of silver.

His mother appeared of average height, but her erect carriage gave the illusion of height. Her maroon traveling gown was set off by a wide hat with soft gray chiffon streamers tied in a bow under her chin. A delicate pink ostrich feather jauntily flew from the brim. However, she wasn't looking around at all. Her total attention was given to the very unhappy baby in her lap. From where she was standing Meghan could hear Bonnie's cries and the woman's frustrated voice. Conner smiled reassuringly, but it was dimmed by his futile attempts to calm Bonnie. Miss Bonnie was having none of it. With spine bowed, head thrown back, and little arms flying, she told the world she didn't want to sit in this stranger's lap.

"There, there, little one," the woman soothed. "Conner, whatever is the matter with her?"

"She doesn't know you, Mother," Conner's father answered for him. "You need to give her time."

The woman looked up and, seeing Meghan standing there, softly replied, "Oh, dear. We're making a frightful first impression, Harry."

Conner stepped from the buggy and, without saying a word, took Bonnie from his mother's lap and walked to Meghan. The moment Bonnie saw Meghan, she stopped crying and leaned out of Conner's arms, leaving Meghan no choice but to grab her.

"You little vixen," Meghan whispered into her ear. "You're not supposed to play favorites, especially not now."

Bonnie looked up at her, gave her famous two-teeth grin, and said, "Mmmmm-mmmm." She waited, her blue eyes round with expectancy for Meghan to praise her.

"Conner," the woman called from the buggy, "is she saying Mama?" She seemed aghast at the possibility.

"No!" both Meghan and Conner answered.

"I . . . I've been trying to teach her how to say 'Grandma,' but 'mmmm-mmmm' is as good as I've been able to get." Meghan quietly offered the explanation.

She stepped closer to Conner, needing his strength. All the while her mind busily berated herself for not taking time to pin back her unruly hair and to take off her frosting-stained apron. Why, oh, why, hadn't she just looked to see who it was before rushing out the door?

As if reading her mind, Conner smiled at her and, giving her a slow wink, said, "You look lovely, my Meghan."

His voice was soft and for her alone. Then he put an arm around her shoulders, feeling her tremble as he led her to the buggy.

"Mother, Father, I'd like you to meet Meghan O'Reiley."

Meghan shifted the baby in her arms. "How do you do, Mr. and Mrs. Hendrickson? Please call me Meghan. I hope your trip was uneventful."

Mrs. Hendrickson smiled and nodded. Mr. Hendrickson answered for both of them. "It's very nice to meet you, Meghan, and, yes, our trip went quite well. It's too far though." He gave a meaningful look at Conner. "Too far indeed."

"Quite," Mrs. Hendrickson said, her ostrich feather bobbing in confirmation. "I'm exhausted."

"It appears our granddaughter knows you quite well, Meghan," Mr. Hendrickson said.

Before Meghan could respond, Conner broke in. "Meghan helped me through Bonnie's teething crisis. I was certain Bonnie was seriously ill, but Meghan knew what was wrong and what to do to ease Bonnie and her angry father." He ruffled Meghan's hair, a gesture that wasn't lost on his mother or father.

The silence that greeted his statement was loud.

"Say, young lady," Mr. Hendrickson finally said, breaking the uneasy atmosphere with a mischievous look that Meghan had seen before on his son's face, "would that by any chance be cake icing you're wearing on your apron?"

Meghan glanced down, and a rosy flush swept her face. "I believe it is, Mr. Hendrickson."

"What kind of icing?"

"Seven-minute." She was puzzled at his question.

"Oh, my." He rolled his eyes. "Seven-minute icing. My grandmother used to make it. What kind of cake?"

"Harry," Mrs. Hendrickson cautioned, "you quit badgering that poor girl." She turned toward Meghan. "You'll have to forgive Harry, Meghan. He has a terrible sweet tooth."

"Huh? I just like a little something sweet every now and then. Tops off a meal."

"Uh-huh. Well, then, you certainly wouldn't be interested in a little something sweet now, since there's no meal to top off," she said saucily. The bond between the two of them was apparent. Also apparent was the delight they from baiting each other.

"Now, Mother," he pleaded, but the sparkle was still in his eye, "it's teatime. Isn't that right, young lady?"

Meghan liked him already. She could see so much of Conner in him. "Absolutely, Mr. Hendrickson. It most definitely is teatime. And, just so you know, the seven-minute icing is my granny's recipe too." A smile creased her mouth, a smile that was full of welcome and delight in the man's teasing. A smile that endeared her to the two people in the buggy.

"Well, let's don't sit here. Let's go inside and see if your granny's recipe is as good as my, uh, my granny's." He chuckled over the last word. "And before we continue, let's get a couple of things straight." He attempted a stern look. "The name's Harry. I'm Mr. Hendrickson to my business associates and to people I don't care to befriend. You don't fit into either category. You've become important to my son and to my granddaughter. So, by golly, you'll be important to me."

Meghan's eyes filled with tears, but before she could think of an appropriate way to thank him, Mrs. Hendrickson started talking.

"Harry is absolutely right, as always," she said, patting her husband's arm. "We simply cannot stand on formalities. My name is Holly. I was born December twenty-second, so in the Christmas spirit, I was named Holly. Holly and Harry. Sounds like a theater billing, doesn't it?" She smiled, and two dimples danced at the sides of her mouth. Two dimples exactly like Conner's.

"I . . . I don't know what to say. I've been so anxious, uh, I've been worried . . ."

"She's been worried you wouldn't like her," Conner said, touching the tip of her nose with one finger. "But I knew you would. No one could help but like my Meghan."

His parents' raised eyebrows weren't noticed by either Meghan or Conner. For a moment there was only the two of them. It was a moment of unspoken love.

A cough from Harry brought them back to the present.

"I'm forgetting my manners," Meghan apologized. "Please, won't you come inside and let me make you welcome with"—she smiled at Harry—"a big piece of cake and some tea?"

"Now, that's an offer I don't intend to pass on. Mother?" He held his hand out to assist Holly from the buggy.

"I agree. It is an offer we definitely won't pass on. However, I would like to have a cup of coffee. Do you have such a thing, Meghan? I have lived in England for most of my life, and while I like an occasional cup of tea, I simply adore my cup of coffee . . . any time of the day and"—she smiled—"especially with a big piece of cake."

Meghan laughed in delight. "Two big pieces of cake, one cup of coffee, and one cup of tea. No, let's make that four big pieces of cake, three cups of coffee, and one cup of tea. Miss Bonnie, however, will have milk with her cake."

Chapter Nineteen

Meghan never realized how much she had missed having another woman to talk to. Oh, she knew she missed Granny—knew it every day of her life. A woman to chat with about mundane happenings, a woman to share a cup of coffee with, was a joy Meghan had been denied until Marybeth came into her life. Still, Marybeth was so busy with her husband and small son, Meghan felt that to steal much of her time for idle visiting was an imposition. Meghan limited her visits and consequently was often lonely. Holly might fill that void.

Over cake and drinks she and Conner outlined their plan for using both homes to make the visitors comfortable. And, as Conner had predicted, both parents were more than willing. In fact, Conner's mother giggled like a young girl and said it would be as if she and Harry were courting again. Conner's father didn't seem to share her pleasure in this thought, but Meghan saw him give his wife a wink and a quick squeeze.

When it was time for Meghan to feed the chickens and do the rest of the evening chores, Conner said he'd help. Holly and Harry said they'd sit in her cozy kitchen and get to know their granddaughter. Bonnie was busy showing off her new crawl-scoot method of locomotion. She was a happy baby, totally at ease in Meghan's home.

Later, when Meghan started supper, Holly grabbed one of Meghan's aprons, rolled up her sleeves, and dug right in.

The cabin filled with talk, laughter, and stories of Conner as a little boy. It was obvious he'd been the apple of their eye. It was also obvious he'd been quite mischievous. Meghan loved listening to their stories and fell in love with the little boy as well as with the man. She acknowledged the love but also acknowledged the pain it brought her. She tried to push the knowledge away as quickly as possible, but still it left a dark cloud of ache around her heart. She couldn't have him, but for now she could enjoy him and his delightful parents.

Conner and his father left for Conner's cabin and bed after Harry had said he was fearful of falling asleep in his tea. Holly too looked exhausted. Meghan showed her what few amenities her cabin offered, but by now she was comfortable enough not to feel embarrassment about having so little. Holly exclaimed over Mrs. Black's quilt, which Meghan had put on her guest's bed. And after she helped Meghan get a tired Bonnie dressed in her nightgown and tucked into a special bed they'd made for her, she turned down her own bedcovers and crawled in. Meghan was sure Holly was asleep as soon as she blew out the lamp.

The next morning, Conner and his father came by to pick up Holly and Bonnie. Conner had a tour of the mine planned and tried to coax Meghan into accompanying them.

Though curious to see for herself the conditions Emery had described, Meghan refused, stating her promise to visit to Marybeth and several other recovering patients she needed to follow up on. They all quit coaxing when she told them she'd have a supper of fried chicken ready when they returned. In fact, Harry was so bold as to caution her to spend as little time as necessary on her calls so she would be sure to have time to fix that chicken dinner. He also told her his favorite piece of chicken and enlisted her help in guarding it from anyone else, especially Conner, who was also partial to that piece. She laughed and assured him he could count on her. Conner pretended to pout. She waved them off with a lightness in her heart, thrilled with this special family and their more than special son.

Meghan enjoyed her visit with Marybeth. Then she managed to talk her into taking a much needed nap while she and Jimmy went outside for a walk. When she returned to the cabin, it was to find a rested Marybeth. Together they discussed the happenings in Pig Eye Gulch over a cup of coffee while Jimmy napped.

More new families were moving into the valley each

week. Marybeth had heard there was a minister due in town any day now. Neither one had any idea where church services would be held, since the largest structure was the mess tent Conner had set up for his miners.

Later in the day, Meghan stopped by Roberts' General Store. The store served as a natural gathering place in Pig Eye Gulch, and she was sure that if anyone had any information about the new minister, it would be Mrs. Roberts. And she was just as sure Mrs. Roberts would willingly, if not gladly, share it with her. She had an ulterior motive for stopping by the store. Several weeks ago she had ordered something special from a catalog; it should be in by now, and she couldn't wait to get it home.

The bell over the door rang merrily as Meghan walked inside. Since Conner had confronted Mr. Roberts, Marybeth could count on his giving her wide berth.

Mrs. Roberts hurried forward, a smile on her face.

"It's—or I should say they?—are here, Meghan. I was so hoping you'd come in this week." She gave a shudder. "Having them in the back of the store and hearing them gives me the shivering shudders. I can't imagine why you would want to undertake a project of this nature. It's certainly not one I'd choose." She sniffed. "And most women would agree, I might add. Still, you have been raised differently than other young ladies your age. However, I feel it my duty to caution you on this project, Meghan. It could be dangerous. Even," she said, lowering her voice, "deadly." She crossed her arms over her chest.

"Thank you, Mrs. Roberts." Meghan's eyes shone with excitement. "Oh, I can't wait to get them home." She was as eager to get her special order home as Mrs. Roberts was to get it out of the store.

"Well, you'll have to have some help getting it to your cabin. It's too much for you to carry or cart there in your wagon. And I wouldn't advise stirring things up too much, if you know what I mean."

Meghan appreciated all Mrs. Roberts had done in providing her with the catalog and the ordering. Still, couldn't help but notice that Mrs. Roberts took a certain pleasure in her warnings and might possibly be disappointed should her forecast of trouble come to naught.

Feeling ashamed of herself for those thoughts, Meghan asked if she had heard anything about the minister coming to Pig Eye Gulch.

"Indeed I have. Reverend Mullen." She puffed up with pride at her knowledge. "Reverend Mullen is a bachelor. He came into the store and introduced himself to Mr. Roberts and me. Quite handsome." She leaned over to confide this to Meghan. "Quite handsome indeed. A bit on the thin side, but that could be remedied with some good home cooking. Mind you, Meghan, there'll be several young ladies in the gulch offering meals and their company to Mr. Mullen." She waited expectantly for Meghan to respond. Gossip like this was prime.

"I couldn't agree more, Mrs. Roberts. There's nothing like good home cooking. As for the young ladies, I couldn't speak for that except to say that Pig Eye Gulch will certainly offer a warm hand of hospitality to any man of God."

It wasn't the answer Mrs. Roberts wanted, so she quickly shifted to another topic that might of interest.

"And how is your company—or should I say Mr. Hendrickson's?—company? I understand they're staying at your home?"

"Mrs. Hendrickson and Bonnie are. Conner's cabin is too small for everyone." Meghan kept her answer short, not wanting to encourage Mrs. Roberts or to add any grist to her gossip mill.

"Conner? So, you and Mr. Hendrickson are on a first-name basis?" She rushed on, not waiting for an answer. "Well, Meghan, I wouldn't go setting my cap for Mr. Hendrickson if I were you. He's not of our kind. Too rarified for common folk. Mind you, I like him, and he's doing great things for Pig Eye Gulch. But I would be surprised should he be around long. Nosiree, he'll return to England with his mother and father. That little girl needs a mother, and I'm quite sure his parents will have a say in who that will be. Wouldn't surprise me at all—no, not at all—should they already have someone picked out for their son." She waited with an all-knowing smile on her face for Meghan's reply.

"I wouldn't know, Mrs. Roberts." Meghan prayed her voice wouldn't betray her and give Mrs. Roberts a glimpse of how those words hurt, even though they mirrored her own thoughts. She glanced toward the door and escape. "I'll not keep you any longer, Mrs. Roberts.

I'll ask Conner and his father if they would be so good as to pick up my supplies tonight. I won't leave them longer than absolutely necessary. You have been more than helpful, and I appreciate it."

"I'm glad to do what I can, Meghan. I'll also let you be the first to know when Mr. Mullen arrives. A minister might be agreeable to getting to know a young lady of your background. However, Meghan, since you don't have a mother, and now not even your granny, I feel I would be shirking my duty as an elder female acquaintance not to tell you that your independent manner and your unladylike, uh"—she fumbled for the correct word—"endeavors, such as this last project of yours"—and here she pointed to the back room—"will have to stop. No man wants his wife to be involved in pursuits of a—shall we say?—masculine nature. I hope I haven't offended you. We all admire the work you do to assist in our various illnesses and needs. Someday this valley will have a real physician. It's a shame the nearest one is in Lewistown. Until then, you fill the need, but I'm quite sure your husband would not want that to continue."

Meghan took a deep breath. Conner wouldn't do for her, and now maybe even a minister wouldn't. Mrs. Roberts didn't mean to be spiteful, but her words hurt nonetheless.

"Thank you again, Mrs. Roberts. I . . . I'll take into consideration all you've said."

She left the store, her step not as light as when she'd entered. "Darn it to heck and back," she muttered to herself, red curls bouncing. Well, she would not let

Mrs. Roberts mar this beautiful day. Conner and his family would be back before long, and she had them to look forward to. Them and, of course, a fried chicken dinner.

Chapter Twenty

Dinner was a huge success. The chicken helped, but the success was in the sharing. Meghan, who had never had a family, was content to sit back and listen to the conversation and banter that filled the cabin.

Conner shared about the day's tour, and through his eyes Meghan could see it all. He was so proud of his mine and all the improvements he'd made. As Conner talked, Meghan stole a look at Harry and saw nothing but pride on his face for what his son was doing.

"Meghan," Harry said, "did Conner tell you about his latest technology?"

"No, I didn't," Conner said with a smile, "but I'm going to now. I was hoping to show it to her, not tell."

"Ooops." His father laughed. "Spilled the beans, did I?"

"Not at all. I still intend to show it off to her." He

turned his full gaze on Meghan. "What my father is alluding to is the telegraph machine I've installed."

Meghan's eyes were shinning. "A telegraph? Mr. Morse's telegraph machine? Oh, Conner, how exciting."

"It is, isn't it?" Conner was like a little boy at Christmas. "I've been wanting to install one since I read about Mr. Morse's success in Washington, D.C."

"Wasn't he awarded thirty thousand dollars by the government to run that line between Washington, D.C. and Baltimore, Maryland?" Meghan asked.

"You know about that?" Conner asked, his voice full of admiration.

"Some." She felt discomfort as all eyes were now focused on her. "We heard about it at Miss Fairchild's, and I was so interested, I did some more reading. Mr. Morse ran the line, and to prove it would work, he quoted, 'What hath God wrought?' "

"That's exactly right. Messages are transmitted on the wires from the transmitter to the receiver. But one of the problems is, every twenty miles there has to be a relay installed that will repeat the signal and send it on another twenty miles. The line can be costly, and the sender has to learn Mr. Morse's code. The receiver must know it too."

"Conner," his mother asked, "how exactly does this 'Morse code' work? I find it all terribly fascinating. Why, you could send and receive a message in a matter of days."

"Hours," Conner answered. "Morse code represents electric impulses. To be more exact, it's a series of long and short impulses—called dots and dashes—triggered by the pressure of the operator's finger on the telegraph key. Used correctly, they become an alphabet to spell out a message. Of course, you have to be trained in sending the correct dots and dashes."

"You know all about this?" Meghan exclaimed.

Conner shrugged and gave a small laugh. "I don't pretend to know *all* about it, but I am qualified as a telegraph operator."

"You are?" Meghan felt as if she were the only one surprised by this confession.

"Since my trip to Helena. In fact, that was the purpose of my trip. I came over to tell you about it the minute I returned, but"—his gaze softened at the memory—"we got caught up in other matters, and I left without doing so." He paused, then went on. "I've wanted to do this for a long time, but for one reason or another, the timing was always off. The wires are run from here to the next qualified telegrapher in Lewistown. Meghan, I feel as if I've opened the door to the rest of the world. We're not so isolated here anymore!" The words were spoken to her and her alone. He wanted her to share his pride of accomplishment. It was as if he needed her approval, because it meant so much to him.

"I'm so proud of you, Conner! Just think what this will mean to Pig Eye Gulch." She smiled widely. "It's amazing to think of the ways your telegraph can be used. Oh, I can't wait to see it. I wish now I'd gone with you today."

"There'll be another day, my Meghan." He reached

across the table and touched the tips of her fingers with his.

"Harry sent a message," Holly volunteered. "With Conner's help, of course."

"That I did," Harry said proudly. "I sent one to our mine office in Lewistown. I believe I could pick up that Morse code in no time."

"I don't doubt it." Conner laughed. "Anyway, enough about our day. What went on in yours, Meghan? How's Marybeth?"

"Marybeth is fine. Tired, anxious, but fine." She smiled. She turned to Holly to offer an explanation. "Marybeth is a friend who's expecting her second baby. I'm guessing, but I wouldn't be surprised if it made its appearance next week or so. I should say 'her' appearance, because I don't believe Marybeth will have it any other way. It's a girl, she's informed me, and I'm beginning to believe she's right." Then she turned back to Conner.

"I was in the general store today, and—" she paused, seeing Conner's raised eyebrows—"Everything was fine, Conner," she reassured him, "I'm going to need your help, if you wouldn't mind, picking up some items I've ordered. I'm sorry, but I volunteered you and your buggy."

"I'd be glad to help. You know that." His look was piercing, his eyes dark with intensity. He sensed that Meghan had been hurt in some way today. She was covering it as best she could, but she couldn't quite hide the pain in her eyes. He knew too that whatever it was, she would keep it to herself, refusing the protection he wanted to give.

"Thank you. But here's the problem. It has to be done tonight. Mrs. Roberts is more than anxious to get it out of her back room." She chuckled. "I should say she's anxious to get it out of her building. If she could have, she would have loaded it onto my back and sent me on my way this afternoon."

"Meghan," Conner asked apprehensively yet with delight in this woman, "what did you order?"

Three pairs of eyes watched for her answer.

She licked her lips, stalling, hoping they would understand. She'd had enough ridicule to last a lifetime. And, for the first time in her life, she desperately wanted and needed a certain man's approval.

"Meghan?" Conner asked again, his voice playfully coaxing. His eyes never left hers. He gave her his unconditional approval and acceptance.

She caught her bottom lip between her teeth and straightened her back, confidence flowing through her once again.

A mischievous look danced across her face. "Bees!"

Three voices chimed in as a choir. "Bees?"

"Uh-huh," she replied, enjoying every minute of her revelation. "Bees. I plan on beekeeping."

"Meghan," Holly exclaimed, "you are absolutely amazing! Would you mind if I poured us all another cup of coffee and tea?" She flashed Harry a warm look. "I can hardly wait to hear all about this, and a cup of coffee will only enhance the telling."

"By all means." Meghan laughed. "And while you're doing, that I'll cut the apple pie—unless the men are too full?"

"Apple pie!" Harry rolled his eyes. "You'll be the death of me, Meghan. But"—he chuckled—"I'll go a happy man. Let me rephrase that: a fat, happy man."

A few minutes later, over steaming coffee and tea and generous slices of pie, Meghan was ready to talk about her bees. Even Bonnie quietly waited, munching bites of pie as she sat in her grandmother's lap.

"Okay, Meghan," Holly said, feeding Bonnie a small bite, "we're all ears. Tell us about your bees."

"Well," Meghan said, her smile wide with pleasure, "as I said, I ordered all the supplies, plus the bees." She grinned wickedly. "Mrs. Roberts was not quite fully aware of what would be arriving at her store. I was assured by the supplier that I will have everything needed to start my hive, including worker bees, drones, and, of course, the queen. She lays thousands of eggs a day and feeds certain ones something called royal jelly. The worker bees are all female, but only the queen lays eggs. The drones . . . well, the drones are for, uh, for . . ." Meghan lowered her voice and blushingly said, "Reproduction."

"Why, you are very informed, Meghan," Holly said admiringly. "Do go on."

"I'm not all that informed, but I will be. I ordered a copy of the book, *The Pleasure and Art of Apiculture.*"

"Apiculture?" Harry asked.

"That's what beekeeping is called. Until Mr.

Langstroth's—Mr. Lorenzo L. Langstroths's—amazing discovery, the only way we knew to get honey was to kill the bees and cut out the honeycomb from the hive. This was called harvesting," she explained. "But Mr. Langstroth discovered what he calls bee space."

"Bee space?" Conner said. "Now, what exactly is bee space?"

"Bee space involves separating frames in a hive from each other by a very small gap—only enough room for a single bee to pass through. The bees respect this space and leave it free. Then, when it's time to harvest the honey, you simply remove the frames. They don't have to be cut free, and the bees don't have to be killed."

It was quiet around the table as each person reflected on her words.

"Am I boring you?" Meghan asked fearfully. "I tend to get carried away with my projects."

"Absolutely not."

"Oh, no, not at all."

"Go ahead, my Meghan. Tell us more."

She flushed. "Well, the main box is called a super, and each super, can hold ten wooden frames. Can you believe that one colony of bees can produce eighty pounds of honey and twenty to forty pounds of wax? I'll have plenty of honey for myself and to give away as well as to sell. I can even sell the wax for candlemaking. I've also read that beeswax is excellent for waterproofing."

"Meghan," Holly said, her voice laced with concern, "isn't this a bit dangerous? I mean, can't you be stung? I do think it quite exciting, and I admire your business acumen, but I fear it—a hive of bees angry, at you for stealing their honey. I have visions of a cloud of buzzing bees circling your head, stingers ready."

The men chuckled at the picture.

"Mother's right, you know. It is a risky business. What about this, Meghan? I'm sure you've thought it through. While I may not have known you long, I still have formed an opinion. And it's a good one," he said, smiling. "You're not the type to attempt anything without proper research and without a good deal of thought. Am I right?"

"Thank you, Harry. I hope I always live up to your opinion of me. I have given this a great deal of thought. In addition to the bees, the super, and the frames, I also ordered the proper clothing. I will always wear something of a light color, as darker colors tend to irritate bees and make them want to sting. I will have a hat with a wire veil. The mesh wire will keep the bees away from my face. Gloves and high boots will keep them from crawling up my arms or down into my shoes. When I harvest the hive, I'll use a smoker. It burns wood scraps and quiets or makes the bees drowsy so I can quickly get in and remove the filled honeycombed frames. I am trusting this has all arrived. I'm sure my bees will want to be released from their temporary captivity in Mrs. Roberts' store. They're eager to start foraging for nectar and pollen."

"Where will you put your hive?" Conner asked.

"In the middle of the south meadow. I want to place it where it will have shade from the summer sun and yet where it will stay warm. The hive has to be at ninety-three degrees. If the sun doesn't keep it warm, the bees will have to burn honey to stay warm. The meadow is full of alfalfa, dandelions, and some goldenrod. These plants provide excellent forage for the bees. However, I will probably have to feed them this winter, as I'm getting a late start." She took a sip of her lukewarm coffee and smiled up at them. "I've rattled on something terrible, monopolizing the entire conversation."

"At our request," Holly said.

"Meghan, let's go get that order of yours. I can hardly wait to see you in that hat and fancy wire veil, a smoker in one hand and a piece of honeycomb in the other." Conner's eyes crinkled, and the two dimples magically appeared at the side of his mouth, evidence of his pleasure in teasing her. "But there is one small favor I'd like to ask of you. In fact, it's becoming more and more important to me as I think about it."

"Of course, Conner. What is it?"

"Could we somehow manage to let a couple of your angry honey bees loose in the Robertses' back room? I believe two to three would do the trick. Could you spare them?"

Chapter Twenty-one

The sun was barely up the next morning when Meghan, book in hand, stood before the equipment spread all around her. Conner stood by her side, reading over her shoulder. From the looks of the items surrounding them, the task seemed daunting.

The meadow was quiet, the early-morning hush broken only by an occasional bird.

The chill of the autumn dawn whispered around them.

"Do you think the bees will be drowsy? The book says they move slower when it's cool."

"Well," Conner said, "it's cool, all right." He put an arm around her shoulders, feeling her shiver in the morning air. He welcomed any excuse to touch her. He smiled down at her. At this moment, standing there beside her, sharing the morning sun as it warily peeped over the mountains, Conner knew true contentment. He knew

211

there was no place he'd rather be than here in Pig Eye Gulch alongside Meghan O'Reiley.

He wasn't that sure, however, about the beekeeping project at hand. But one look at Meghan's determined face, and he knew there would be no putting off the task at hand. Her bees were to have a home—today. He reluctantly removed his arm from around her and bent down to the assembled items of beekeeping.

Meghan read to him from the book, giving directions as he hammered the super together. By the time it came to inserting the frames into the super, Conner was as engrossed in the project as Meghan. Both lost track of time and welcomed the warmth of the sun on their backs.

When the hive was finished, set under the big willow tree, empty and waiting, Conner turned to Meghan. "Well, my Meghan, it's all yours. There are some—I hope sleepy—bees waiting for their new home. Are you ready?"

Meghan looked small and lost in her large beekeeping hat and veil. The gloves swallowed her hands. "I'm ready." Her voice quavered, but only for a moment. "Oh, Conner, would you think me silly if I confessed to being a bit fearful of this next step?"

"Not at all. I'm a bit fearful too," he confessed with a laugh.

With no further ado, Meghan took a gulp of air, squared her shoulders, and, following the instructions in *The Pleasure and Art of Apicuture*, she slowly, gently, and with many silent prayers, transferred the imprisoned bees to their new home.

Putting the lid on the super, she stepped back and smiled through her veil at Conner, who stood a respectful distance from the hive. Ever so slowly she backed away, her eyes never leaving the hive.

Then they both waited, watching, not speaking, barely breathing, as first one, then two bees came out of the hive and swirled a lazy circle in the air. They flew the short distance to the goldenrod and settled on first one stem and then another. Catching a faint buzzing sound, Meghan heard a melody more beautiful than any symphony. These were her bees, and this was their home. She had done it. She looked up at the man beside her, shirtsleeves rolled up, forearms revealing his sinewy strength. He had helped build her dream.

"Thank you, Conner," she said softly. "I couldn't have done this without you."

He gently lifted the veiled hat from her head and laid it beside her feet. Then, tucking an errant wisp of hair behind her ears, he bent and gently placed a kiss on her upturned nose.

"Well, you are now an official beekeeper." His voice was husky with emotion. He was so proud of her. So proud and so in love with this amazing woman. He started to speak, to tell her again of his love, then stopped, reminding himself of his pledge to be patient. He would let her go on thinking friendship was all they'd ever have, but just for a while longer.

"If you think you can leave these fine fellows alone, let's go back to the house and see if my father has made it out of bed to join us for breakfast. I left while he was still snoring. I know Mother will be awake. Bonnie will see to that. We'll leave the bees to settle in and start house-keeping." He chuckled. "Then we'll come back every few hours."

"How did you know that was exactly what I was think-ing?"

"I'm beginning to know you, my Meghan. And it doesn't take a mind reader to know that your bees will never be too far from your watchful eye."

Conner was right. Holly and Bonnie were indeed up. Holly had mastered the kitchen range enough to put a pot of coffee on to boil. The aroma drifted out the cabin door and into the yard. It was the first thing to greet them as they stepped inside. The second greeting, or lack thereof, was from Conner's father. Instead of his usual, amiable smile and a call of hello, he gave a dismal shake of his head and a mumbled grunt. His hand gently cupped a swollen jaw.

"Harry's tooth is acting up again," Holly informed them, shaking her head sympathetically. "He's had trou-ble before but refuses to let the doctor pull it." She turned back toward the ailing man. "I was afraid something like this would happen, Harry. That tooth has got to come out!"

Harry's mumbled "No!" left no doubt as to his opinion.

"Harry," Meghan said softly, "would you let me take a look at your tooth? Perhaps I can suggest something that will give you some relief. It may well need to be pulled, but we might be able to delay that ordeal for a while."

"Mmmm," Harry replied, and he gently pulled the side of his mouth open, giving Meghan enough room to peer in.

"Oh, Harry, I can see exactly which one it is. The gum around it is swollen and red." She stepped back and met his hopeful look. "I think I can help."

"Meghan, would you? We'd appreciate anything you could do." Holly was quick to accept her offer, not giving Harry a chance to reply.

"The first thing we're going to do is stun the tooth pain with oil of cloves. I'll put a couple drops directly onto the sore tooth. That should relieve the pain. It will also act against the infection. We do have to be careful using clove oil, as it has been known to irritate the gums, and we sure don't want you to have any more irritation than you already have. That's why, in between applying the oil of clove, I'll be making a decoction of sesame seed. I'll have to boil this and let it cool, but I think you'll have relief from the clove before we use the sesame seed."

Meghan was the epitome of confidence as she delivered her prescribed course of action. She didn't expect, nor did she receive, any hesitant looks or questions. Her healing ability was readily accepted.

It was with complete self-assurance that she gathered her herbs and started the sesame seed concoction to boil. While this was boiling, she took the essence of cloves to where Harry sat and proceeded to apply it to directly to the sore tooth. The smell of cloves was pleasant and somewhat reassuring. Harry closed his eyes, anticipating the possibility of relief.

"Meghan," Holly said, "your bees. We completely forgot to ask how the bees' house and their transfer went."

"It went fine," Conner answered for her. "Meghan transferred those bees as if she'd been doing it all her life. I had to coax her away, or she'd still be up there waiting for us to serve her breakfast at the hive."

"Oh, you! I expected no such a thing. Conner did a beautiful job constructing the super, Holly. I couldn't have done it by myself. And even if I did manage to do so, it would have taken me weeks, not one morning."

Holly smiled at their mutual admiration.

"Have you forgotten about me?" a voice interrupted.

"Harry! Already? You're feeling relief already?" Holly went to her husband.

Harry gave a small smile, not wanting to test the new-found relief. "Yes, I am. It's amazing. Oh, there's still some pain, but not the throbbing I was experiencing. How often can we apply the cloves, Meghan? I don't want to wait too long."

Meghan chuckled. "I left the bottle near you, Harry. Feel free to apply another small amount, but put it directly on the tooth. The sesame seed mix will be cooled and ready soon, and we can alternate it with the cloves." She motioned to the cooling concoction. "While we're waiting, how about some breakfast? I don't know about all of you, but working in the brisk morning air gave me an appetite. What about you, Conner?"

He smiled at her, but before he could reply, Harry answered. "I do believe I could eat a soft-boiled egg. Would that be permissible, Dr. Meghan?"

Meghan nodded. "Only one, Harry?"

He chuckled. "Better make that two or three. I'm getting spoiled by your fresh eggs and pancakes."

"Pancakes?" Holly said, puzzled. "No one said anything about pancakes."

"They didn't?" Harry said with a twinkle in his eye. "I could have sworn Meghan asked me if I wanted a pancake with my eggs."

"You may have a pancake." Meghan laughed. "But no syrup."

"No syrup?" he asked, horrified.

"Not unless you want that tooth to start hurting again. For the time being we need to keep anything away from it that might trigger the pain. The sugar in the syrup would do just that."

"Meghan," Harry said, "I'm impressed with your knowledge about healing and the herbs you use. Didn't you or Conner tell me that you learned everything from your grandmother?"

"I did," she said, a loving look crossing her face. "Granny practiced healing with herbs for many years here in Pig Eye Gulch."

"Many years, huh?"

"Yes. Why?"

"Well, I do believe I know a little something of your granny, Meghan."

"What could you possibly know?" Conner asked, surprised.

"Well, I remember a story that was told me by Conner's grandfather. It's quite interesting, and I'd be glad to share it with all of you."

"Just a moment, Harry," Holly said. "We can't get breakfast, feed Bonnie, and do complete justice to your story. Let's wait until we've eaten and then enjoy our coffee while you talk. I have to confess, Harry, sometimes you just amaze me. I've yet to find something that you don't know a little bit about."

Harry preened under her praise. "Well, I don't know for sure if this pertains to Meghan, but I'll just bet it does. After breakfast it is, then."

There was no time lost getting breakfast ready. Conner took Bonnie off their hands and dressed her. He placed her on a chair, tying her in place with a dishcloth, then proceeded to feed her a little bit of egg and pancake.

There was little conversation while they ate, and as soon as breakfast was over, dishes were cleared and put to soak in a large dishpan. Meghan poured the coffee, a bit tense. What could Harry possibly know about Granny? He had been in England while Granny was alive. This was his first trip to the Big Snowy Mountains and Pig Eye Gulch. Still, she had no doubt he wouldn't have mentioned the story without confidence that it was connected to her granny.

Conner pulled back a chair beside him and smiled at her to sit down. His curiosity and concern was melded with hers. Anything pertaining to Meghan and her life was now of supreme interest to him.

"We're ready, Harry," Holly said. "Let's hear your story."

"Mind you," he cautioned, "I may not have all the facts. But I have been mulling this over during breakfast, and I'm even more convinced it pertains to you, Meghan. It would seem that there was an outbreak of influenza at one of your grandfather's mines," he said, looking at Conner. "Your grandfather was desperate for a doctor, but, of course, the camp had none. He was told of a woman who lived in an adjacent valley, reputed to be wise in the ways of healing with herbs."

"Granny," Meghan breathed.

Harry smiled. "I don't doubt that for a moment. I never connected the story with you, Meghan. In fact, I'd forgotten it until this blasted tooth acted up and you stepped in. So, as I was saying, my father went to the woman's home and told her of the epidemic. She dropped everything and accompanied him to the mining camp. He said she was tireless, caring for the stricken miners and their families. My father was quite impressed with her. He was also impressed by the fact that she asked nothing for her help but left it up to him to give her what he wanted, if anything. He gave her a tour of the mine and showed her his prized homing pigeons. As far as I know, when she returned to her valley, he had no further contact with her." He looked at Meghan and saw the tears in her eyes. "I'm sorry,

Meghan. I feel bad that I even brought this up. I hope I didn't disappoint you."

"Oh, no, Harry, you didn't. I get emotional thinking about Granny and all she did. It's a beautiful story. Now it's my turn. If you will excuse me"—she looked around the table—"I'd like to share something with you. It's something you need to see. It will take me a few minutes to retrieve. I believe it's the second part of your story." She stood up and moved toward the door.

Conner gave his parents a perplexed look and a shrug. "I'll go with you, Meghan."

He followed her outside to the shed, where she got a shovel and then headed to the chicken house. Entering, she startled a few of the hens fluffed on their nest. Feathers flew, and the heavy dust and odor of chicken droppings saturated the air.

"This isn't the most pleasant area or task," she apologized to Conner. "I'd better do it myself. I know what I'm doing." Conner had stepped forward to take the shovel from her hands. She gave him a small smile and started scraping the feathers and droppings away from a corner of the floor. He silently watched her every move. She exposed several planks, then lifted them out, revealing a hollowed out area. Laying the shovel down and dropping to her knees, Meghan reached into the hole and began pulling out fruit jars. Conner stared at the jars, his face mirroring his disbelief. The contents varied. Some were filled with gold nuggets of various sizes, and others were stuffed full of crumbled dollar bills and change. Meghan seemed impervious to the wealth surrounding her as leaned farther into the hole, her hand intently searching the sides and corners.

"Ah, there it is!" she exclaimed as she lifted out a muslin-wrapped package.

Meghan handed it to a speechless Conner and then, as if she handled jars of money every day of her life, began placing them back in the hole. When they were all safely in their hiding place, she laid the planks into place and finished by scraping some of the debris over them for camouflage. She dusted her hands and turned toward him.

"Meghan, do you have any idea what you have hidden here?"

"Uh, well, Conner, not to the exact amount. Of course, some of it is gold, so I'd have to have it weighed and—"

"Meghan," he interrupted, his voice hushed, "you're a wealthy woman. Good Lord, I can't even begin to guess the dollar amount. But putting that aside, what I need to know is, why do you have jars of money hidden in a chicken house?"

"Conner, I am a wealthy woman." She motioned toward the cabin. "I have wealth that money or gold can't buy. Granny left me the jars, and, with them, I have the ability to help others. I get more money returned by the miners I grubstake than I can possibly use. My needs and wants are simple. So, I do as Granny did. I store them here, in my special bank." She chuckled. "Don't you agree they are more than safe?"

"Well, yes. I don't dispute that. It's just—oh, Meghan. My Meghan. People don't usually squirrel jars of money away. They spend it." He reached over and brushed a feather from her hair. "I can understand your reasoning. So help me, as unusual as it is, I understand. It's you. You're a gift, Meghan. And you're right: You have wealth of another nature. Wealth money can't buy. I envy you that wealth."

She reached for the package in his hands and closed her fingers around his. She looked up into the depth of his eyes. "I knew you would understand. You're the only person alive who knows of these jars. The only person I'd want to share this and my inner feelings with. You're a part of my wealth."

They stood there, holding hands and touching hearts. Then, as one they turned and went back to a waiting Holly and Harry.

Chapter Twenty-two

No one had moved from the table except Bonnie. She was happily scooting after Scrapper. When she got close enough to touch him, she'd sit back on her diapered rump and clap her hands in delight. Then they'd take off again. The two babies seemed to have a game all their own.

Holly and Harry watched Meghan and Conner approach. They were quietly waiting for Meghan to reveal the second part of the story.

She lay the muslin-wrapped package on the table and, with great care, proceeded to unwrap it. A collective gasp went up as the two vibrant blue stones were revealed.

"I'll be . . . They're Yogos!" Harry pronounced. "May I?" Not waiting for Meghan's permission, he picked up the two sapphires and held them up to the light. He shook his head, marveling at their combined beauty and luster.

"Perfect, just perfect," he muttered to himself. He raised his eyebrows expectantly at Meghan.

"After hearing your story, I now know these were a gift of appreciation to my granny from your father. I was a little girl when the influenza epidemic hit his mining camp. He did come and ask Granny for her help, just like you said. I went with her the first day but wasn't allowed to stay. Conditions were rough, as were some of the miners. Granny came back, exhausted, with many stories to tell. And, yes, your father did show her his pigeons. In fact, he let her hold one." A smile curved her lips. "Granny was quite impressed." She was quiet for a moment as the memories gathered around her like an afternoon storm. "Your father paid her for her help with these beautiful stones. She knew their value, but she never once planned on keeping them for herself." Meghan closed her eyes, her lashes wet with tears. "She said they were for me. She always talked of someday having them made into earrings." She looked up, and her voice trembled. "Granny said they were precious stones, precious because they reminded her of my sapphire blue eyes." She quoted the woman's words from so many years ago. "After Granny's death, I left them hidden in her special place. It hurt me to see them." She risked a look at Conner. "This is the first time they've seen the light in quite a long time." Then she pushed the two stones toward him. "Here, they're yours."

"Mine?" He was astonished, his brow wrinkling in puzzlement. "Why on earth would you give them to me?"

"Because." Her voice was a whisper in the room. "They belonged to your grandfather."

"Oh, my sweet, that has nothing to do with it. He wanted your granny to have them. He would never have parted with them if he didn't. And from her, with a great deal of love, the gift came to you. She wanted them made up into earrings for her Meghan. Your granny was right, you know—they do match your eyes. Match but could never outshine. I've seen your eyes darken to this shade of blue and sparkle with as much life as these sapphires. Montana blue."

"Conner's right, Meghan," Holly said. She reached across the table and took the girl's slim hands into hers. "It's a beautiful story, and the second part was a grand finish. Conner's finding you, our visit, Harry's story—it was all meant to be." Her smiled warmed those around the table, especially Meghan.

"Meghan," Conner gently said, "on second thought, I would like to accept your sapphires after all."

"Conner!" Holly and Harry said in unison.

"Not for me." He glanced at them. "I would like to accept this treasured gift and have the stones set into the earrings your granny envisioned. I know an excellent jeweler in England who would do them justice. What do you say?"

Meghan worried her lower lip between her teeth. This wasn't going as she had expected. The stones meant so much to her not because of their worth, but because they had belonged to Granny. To have them made into the earrings Granny talked of would be like fulfilling her wish. Still, she couldn't help but feel guilty.

Conner wrapped the sapphires back into their muslin home. "I can see my offer hasn't been fair to you. To ask you to make a decision where only you benefit is asking you to go against your nature. So I'm going to make it for you. Thank you, Meghan, for sharing these with us. They belong in the light, not in a dark hole. I'm going to take the responsibility for doing what I think your granny wanted, and that is to have these set into a pair of earrings." He placed the package in his pocket. Then and only then did he chance a look at Meghan.

Gone were the tears. Instead, her eyes flashed the blue they had all been talking about. "I would like them set in a flower design, Mr. Conner Hendrickson. I'll leave the actual design up to your jeweler, but I want the stones to be the face of a delicate flower."

Conner threw back his head and laughed. "That's my girl. I didn't think you'd let me rule the roost for very long." He reached out and playfully gave a yank to a rebellious curl. "A flower it shall be, my Meghan. A Montana blue flower. Now, a decision has been made. Shall we make another? Don't you think its time we checked on those bees? I understand you and Mother are planning a visit to your friend, Marybeth, later today. So let's go have a look, and you can leave with peace of mind."

"I have an even better idea," Holly interrupted. "You two go check the bees. I'll get Bonnie and me ready to go calling. Then, when you return, Meghan and I will go visit Marybeth while you and Harry do the breakfast dishes." She smiled happily, quite pleased with her suggestion.

The two men looked at each other and groaned. "I think we've been outfoxed, Conner," Harry said. "Outfoxed and outmaneuvered."

It wasn't much later when Meghan and Holly, with Bonnie in tow, left the two men and started down the path. They were going to stop first at the general store. Holly had never been in the store and was eager to see what it offered. Meghan was apprehensive about introducing her to Mrs. Roberts but felt Holly would be more than able to handle the meddlesome woman. She just hoped Mrs. Roberts would refrain from making disparaging remarks about Meghan's upbringing.

They had barely set foot into the store when Mrs. Roberts came toward them, moving so fast that her skirt billowed out behind her. Her usual persimmon expression was replaced by beams of delight.

"Why, Meghan, how nice to see you again, and so soon." The words tumbled over themselves. They may have been directed at Meghan, but her entire being was focused on Holly. Meghan could have walked out of the store for all Mrs. Roberts would have noticed. "You must introduce me to this lovely lady."

"Of course. Mrs. Roberts, I'd like you to meet Holly Hendrickson. Mrs. Hendrickson is Conner's mother. She and Mr. Hendrickson are here visiting from England."

"England," she gushed as if this were the first she'd heard of the visitors. "Oh, I'm delighted, for sure. Simply delighted." She dropped a small curtsey. Holly's eyes flashed with suppressed laughter. "Why, it's like having royalty. Imagine! Visitors from England. Right here in Pig Eye Gulch." She cocked her head to one side, taking in every stitch of Holly's apparel.

"Meghan, shame on you, you naughty girl, for not giving me advance warning of your visit. Why, I would have made myself more presentable. But, indeed, what can you expect?" She turned back to Holly with an expression that said, "Look what I have to put up with." Expecting to see shared understanding, she pulled back her neck, looking like a startled goose at Holly's expression.

"Uh, you know what I mean, Mrs. Hendrickson. You see, Meghan is—"

"Absolutely delightful," Holly broke in. "Why, Mr. Hendrickson and I were both saying what a rare treat it is to find someone of her abilities and manners here in such an isolated area. You know," she said, leaning conspiratorially toward Mrs. Roberts, "Bonnie and I are staying with Meghan, and both of us have come to love and admire her." She turned slightly toward Meghan, momentarily blocking Mrs. Roberts from sight, and gave her a quick wink. "Now, Meghan," she admonished, "don't be modest. You know how we all feel about you."

"Hmmpf," Mrs. Roberts snorted, neither agreeing nor disagreeing with this dismaying tidbit of information. Clearly the conversation wasn't progressing as she had planned. Determined to try again, she gave an insincere smile that was more of a smirk and said, "Yes, well, I suppose she does have her merits. She was sent away to one of the better schools for young ladies. She's quite fortunate for an orphan. Yes, quite. And it certainly should stand her in good stead with Reverend Mullen."

"Reverend Mullen?" Holly asked, puzzled.

Mrs. Roberts preened, eager to enlighten Holly, but before she could get anything out, Meghan interrupted. "Excuse me, Mrs. Roberts, but we really must be going if we're to get to Marybeth's before Jimmy has his nap. Bonnie will be disappointed if she doesn't get to play with him." It was a feeble excuse at best, but Meghan had heard all she ever wanted to hear of the oh, so eligible Reverend Mullen.

"But you just got here," Mrs. Roberts protested. "I haven't even had a chance to show Mrs. Hendrickson around our establishment." Meghan and Reverend Mullen were forgotten. Her "establishment" was now of paramount importance.

Holly, true to her kind nature, smiled back at the woman. "Of course, you must show me around. Meghan, do you think we have time, or should we plan to come back another day?"

Mrs. Roberts jumped on her words like a hen on a June bug. "Another day," she chortled. "Why, yes, another day would be perfect." Her mind was racing, possibilities taking form like clouds in the sky. "I would be better prepared to entertain you, Mrs. Hendrickson." She was already picking out what she'd wear. "In fact, if I could be so bold as to suggest this, I'd like to have a few of the more, uh, suitable ladies in to meet you. We could have tea. I'm quite aware of how you English love your tea." She imparted the last words of wisdom with an upturned face of superiority.

Holly started to correct her by informing her that she was an American. But she stopped short, not wanting to disillusion her. Actually, she didn't want to divulge any more of herself to this gossipy woman than necessary.

"What a lovely idea. Meghan and I would be delighted to attend."

"Meghan?" the woman sputtered, starting to qualify the invitation. She didn't classify Meghan as being her ideal of a "suitable" woman to come to her tea. She opened her mouth, then closed it just as fast, seeing the look on Holly's face. "Why, yes, of course," she muttered weakly. "Meghan."

"You know, Mrs. Roberts . . ." Holly's voice expressed her rising excitement at the idea forming in her head. "Your tea will be a perfect setting to discuss what this valley needs."

"It will?"

"Yes. And so clever of you to think of it."

"I did?"

Holly ignored the woman's questioning response. She had the bit in her mouth and was ready to run. Meghan and Mrs. Roberts didn't know it, but this was Holly Hendrickson at her best.

"This valley needs organizing," she stated emphatically. "And who better to organize it than the women of Pig Eye Gulch?"

"Huh?" Mrs. Roberts was, for once in her life, speechless.

"You mentioned a Reverend Mullen coming."

"Yes, yes, I did."

"Well, he needs a church, doesn't he?"

Mrs. Roberts nodded, not sure what her response should be.

Meghan juggled a restless Bonnie. She was transfixed by what Holly was saying, wondering where on earth she was going with her questions. There was no doubt Holly knew exactly where she was going and how to get there.

"And in just the short time I've been here, I've noticed an abundance of children living here."

"Yes, certainly," Mrs. Roberts agreed.

"Well, then, you need a school."

Meghan smiled. Now she knew where Holly was going. She was leading Mrs. Roberts by the hand, and Mrs. Roberts was following like a horse being led to water. Meghan was filled with admiration for this unique woman. This was the type of woman Conner needed, a woman of Holly's verve and sophistication. A woman of quality. A woman who would be an asset to him. Not, definitely, someone such as herself. And that knowledge saddened her. This was one time Meghan did not want to be right, but right she was. She swallowed the hurt as she willed her thoughts back to the ongoing conversation.

"A school?" Mrs. Roberts parroted. She was still wandering in the desert, searching for direction. And until she knew this elusive direction, she wasn't about to chance voicing anything contrary to what this important visitor expected.

"You do understand, this will be a monumental task?"

"Oh, yes, monumental," Mrs. Roberts said, glad to agree about something.

"But you are just the woman for it."

"Uh, the woman? For the task? But . . . but . . ."

And of course I would expect Meghan to help. She's a natural leader. And, of course, you'll want her friend, Marybeth's, assistance. In fact"—and she scrutinized the store, her manner letting Mrs. Roberts know it was falling short of her discriminating expectations—"I'm not sure this will do. No." She put a finger to her lips. "Not sure at all. Maybe somewhere else would be best."

"Oh, no, Mrs. Hendrickson. This will do. I mean, I will do—no, no, what I mean is . . ." She puffed herself up. "Roberts' General Store will make every effort to do. Uh, Mrs. Hendrickson, just what exactly will it do for?"

"Why, a place to hold your first organizational meeting, Mrs. Roberts. Someplace warm and inviting where all"—and she emphasized the last word—"the women of the town will feel welcome. I'm sure you agree that they must all be part of this endeavor, not just a select few."

"All?" Clearly the possibility of Roberts' General Store being invaded by women she felt beneath her social register dismayed Mrs. Roberts. Still, if that was what Holly Hendrickson expected, then that's what

Holly Hendrickson would get. The meeting most definitely would be held in her store, and she most definitely would run this and all subsequent meetings. She would be the leader in this noble cause. She would have to have assistance, of course. She couldn't be expected to do it all herself. Every army needed a general, and she would be the general of the Pig Eye Gulch's Ladies Club. What a grand name.

"Pig Eye Gulch Ladies Club," she announced imperiously. "Yes, that's what we'll call it, and of course I will be the president, naturally." She glanced at the two women, daring them to contradict her.

"Oh, absolutely!" Holly clapped her hands. "Pig Eye Gulch Ladies Club. A grand name indeed, Mrs. Roberts. Or should I say"—she winked mischievously—"Madame President?"

Mrs. Roberts tried for modesty and fell short. In fact, she fell short of even being sure modesty was needed. Truth was truth.

"Now," she said, warming to her new role, "Mr. Roberts will close the store early, and with a little rearranging, there will be room for us to gather."

"Perfect, don't you think, Meghan?" Holly asked.

Meghan could only nod. She was trying to keep up with Holly and Mrs. Roberts and the quick turn of the events. She found her voice, knowing Holly wanted her to be part of this group. And, the truth was, she wanted to be part of it. "Yes, I do agree, it's perfect. We'll need a church and a school." She laughed in excitement at the changes coming to her valley.

"First things first," snapped Mrs. Roberts, not to be outdone by this chit of a girl. "The meeting should be held soon. Mrs. Hendrickson, would you be so good as to attend?"

"I'd be delighted. You set the date and time." She took hold of Meghan's arm, her action telling Mrs. Roberts that Meghan was someone of value, someone special to Holly Hendrickson. "Meghan and I will be there. We'll bring the tea cakes. I have a recipe from my cook that is simply delectable."

"Why, thank you, Mrs. Hendrickson." Mrs. Roberts tried for nonchalance at the mention of the woman's cook. She must not act surprised or impressed. She must act as if having a cook was common. *Oh, my, wait until she told everyone. What a day this had been. First a visit from Conner Hendrickson's mother from England. And now this turn of events.* She would be the envy of the valley and rightfully so.

"I'll be getting in touch with you and Meghan," Mrs. Roberts added agreeably, her tone of voice regal. Gone was her offer of a tour. There was no time now; she had other fish to fry. She had an organizational meeting to plan. Holly Hendrickson might have a cook, but she—she was president of the Pig Eye Gulch Ladies Club.

Chapter Twenty-three

Marybeth welcomed her visitors. Her home was humble, but her warmth and pleasure in the company of her dearest friend and Meghan's companion filled the small cabin with a cheer that chased away the drabness.

She poured them each coffee and served it in mismatched cups. The cracked one she saved for herself. She put a plate of cookies in front of the visitors and handed two to Jimmy and Bonnie.

"Mmm, these smell wonderful, Marybeth. And still warm. My favorite kind of cookies."

"They are?" asked Marybeth. "You favor sugar cookies?"

"No." Holly laughed. "I favor all cookies, and especially I favor warm-from-the-oven cookies."

Laughter filled the kitchen. And that set the tone of the visit. It was a visit of sharing, planning, and laughter as Meghan and Holly related their visit with Mrs. Roberts.

"Oh, my, no." Marybeth wiped a tear from her eye. "I can just hear her now. Madame President. Still, Mrs. Hendrickson, what a perfect idea and plan. We do need a church, and," she said as she patted her tummy, "we need a school. Our children need every opportunity we can give them."

"I couldn't agree more. And, Marybeth, you must stop calling me Mrs. Hendrickson. I'm Holly to my friends."

"Oh, I-I couldn't," Marybeth stammered, her composure lost. "You're the mother of my husband's boss. The mine's owner. It would be disrespectful."

"No, it would be right. I may be Conner's mother, but I am a person in my own right, and that person has friends who call her by her first name. I'll have it no other way, Marybeth."

Marybeth smiled. "Thank you. Holly it is. I would like very much to be considered your friend. Meghan is a gift, and now I'll add you to my prayers of thanks." She paused, then went on. "Perhaps I'm being too forward, Mrs. Hend—uh, Holly, but won't the school need a teacher?"

"Absolutely. That will be an immense hurdle to jump through, all right. One will have to be found, and then, of course, there will be the issue of pay and a place to hold classes. You ladies of Pig Eye Gulch will be busy. The tasks ahead of you are monumental but not insurmountable." Holly's eyes twinkled.

Meghan and Marybeth sipped their coffee and nibbled

on cookies. The tasks were huge. Holly was right. But along with that acknowledgment, there was an awareness that these tasks were worth attempting. A school and a church were both badly needed.

"I'm a teacher." The still of the room was broken as the words fell from Marybeth's lips.

Meghan and Holly's heads shot up.

"I . . . I am. I am qualified, although I haven't had much experience," she said apologetically. "I married Emery soon after I completed my education, and then Jimmy came along." She laughed. "And Pig Eye Gulch came along not too long after that."

"Marybeth!" Meghan exclaimed. "I never knew . . . you never said." Meghan's face was wreathed in smiles of pride in her friend's accomplishment. "Would you be able to take over teaching with two babies, one new?"

"Oh, Meghan, I would love to try. By the time we find a place to have the school, the new baby will be here. There has to be a way. It would be like a dream come true. I loved it the few weeks I taught." Her face shone with excitement. "You can't imagine the joy of seeing a young face light up as she reads her first word or writes her name. To help a child, well, it's hard to describe what a warmth it gives you inside, what a sense of well-being. Do you think there's a chance they'll allow me to try?"

"I can guarantee you, they will jump at the chance. Anyway, who are 'they'?" Meghan asked with a wide grin on her face. "We're the 'they,' Marybeth. We're the ones who first saw the need, and we're the ones who will help bring it all about."

"I'm so excited!" Marybeth exclaimed. "I thought I couldn't wait until my daughter was born, and now I can't wait until the first day of school. The first day of school. Meghan, did you think we'd ever say that? The first day of school," she repeated in wonderment.

"Now, slow down, you two. Marybeth, calm down and drink your coffee before you have that baby right now," Holly admonished with a laugh. "Meghan, don't let her get any more excited. I'm not eager to help with a birthing today, although I do want to see that baby girl before we go. There's still the matter of a place to hold the classes. Before you two can begin lesson plans, we need to find somewhere large enough."

Meghan shook her head. "I don't think that will be a problem, Holly." Visions of jars of money and gold shimmered in her mind. "I don't think finding a schoolhouse will be a problem. In fact, I predict there will be one built and ready for use by Christmas."

Holly and Marybeth looked at her. "Oh, Meghan, you have such faith. If only it were that easy. Still, we can hope and trust that some way, somehow, we will have our school by then," Marybeth said.

"We will," Meghan reassured them. "Of that I have no doubt. Granny felt education was so important, she sacrificed having me near her so I could attend school. She would agree that money spent for a school was money that came into being for just that reason."

"I don't know how you're so sure, but if you can believe that strongly, why, then, so can I. Of course, we can't forget the church. That's vital to our town. Our town," Marybeth said musingly. "Our town."

Holly was uncharacteristically quiet for rest of the visit. However, Meghan and Marybeth were so full of plans and ideas that this went by without notice. It was later that evening, as they were all gathered for their evening meal, that Holly revealed what had been on her mind. She and Meghan filled the men in on their day. And, Harry and Conner reveled in the story of the women's visit to Roberts' General Store. The men agreed that Holly had handled Mrs. Roberts quite nicely and that the plans for a school and church were most timely.

"Harry, Conner," Holly said, "I have something to say."

"Well, Mother, it would seem you've had nothing but something to say since you got home. You've been full of news. Chattering like a magpie." Harry had a sparkle in his eye as he teased the woman he loved. He was very glad she'd pushed him into making this visit sooner rather than later. He also admitted to himself that he'd never been as content as he'd been these last few weeks. It was as if he had his son back after a long, dismal drought.

"Harry, you behave! What I have to say is important, and I need everyone's full attention."

"You have it, Mother. I shouldn't tease you, but may I say one more thing?"

"Well," she said impatiently, "what is it, Harry?"

"You're mighty pretty when you're this fired up." He

held up a hand to stop her sputtering. "Now, now. Have your say. I've had mine."

Meghan's eyes danced from one to the other, enjoying the love that flowed like a river's current between them. She caught Conner's glance, and their eyes held for a brief moment, sharing their joy.

"As I said"—she gave Harry a warning look—"I have something to say, and it's of great importance. We've discussed a church and a school. And"—she paused, assuring she had their full attention—"I feel Harry and I should donate the church. There. I've said it." And she gave a challenging look around the table, daring anyone to dispute her.

"And," said Harry, his voice booming louder than usual, "I agree."

"You do?" Holly asked.

"Now, Mother, don't act so surprised. Of course I do. Pig Eye Gulch is getting a minister, and a minister needs a church. And we will see that he gets that church. We may have to extend our visit." His eyes danced as an expression of surprised delight filled Holly's face. "But I don't think that will be a problem, do you, my dear?"

"Oh, Harry." She jumped up from her seat, ran around the table to his side, and threw her arms around him. "Of course it won't be a problem, if it won't be for Conner and Meghan. Oh, I've been so dreading going back. I'm just getting to know Meghan and our sweet, sweet Bonnie. Another week or two just wasn't going to be enough."

"What about me, Mother?" Conner asked, attempting to look hurt. "Don't I count?"

"You, my adorable boy, count very much. Without you, we wouldn't have these two ladies in our lives." She left Harry and encircled Conner with her arms, giving him a peck on the cheek. "There now, happy?"

"Yes." He laughed, then looked at Meghan and said, "Very."

"I don't mean to be a rain cloud, but there's still the matter of the school." Harry looked expectantly at Conner, but before he had a chance to respond, Meghan spoke up.

"The school's taken care of."

"It is?" Harry said, surprised.

Conner was silent, watching her, knowing she had something planned.

"Yes," Meghan replied. "Let's just say there's money enough to build the school. Jars of money." She gave Conner a wink.

He smiled back, knowing exactly what she was referring to. His heart felt full to bursting with love for this unselfish woman. She gave back more, much more than she received, and they were all the richer for it.

"Please," Meghan said, "let this be my secret. Holly, you'll have to help me present it to the ladies when the time is right. I would rather no one knows where the money comes from. Could it be from an anonymous donor?"

Holly studied Meghan's face, then said, "Of course.

Conner, Harry, Meghan, a dear departed relative of ours left a small inheritance to be used for education. We have all discussed it and feel a school for Pig Eye Gulch would be the appropriate use of this money. Agreed?" She challenged anyone to contest the newly invented relative.

The two men nodded.

"Thank you, Holly. Thank you for understanding." Meghan looked out the window, and her thoughts left the table and the people seated there. They flew to a special lady showing a young girl jars of money hidden in a chicken house. A lady who had been a friend to others in need. She thought of the miners and the grubstakes, and she thought of the little orphan girl, all nourished by this woman's love. How fitting that the children of her beloved valley should also be nourished by the gift of learning.

Chapter Twenty-four

Several days later Conner walked to the woodshed to check on Lady, and he heard someone talking inside. He recognized his mother and Meghan and started to join them. Not meaning to eavesdrop, he paused when he heard his mother ask Meghan what Mrs. Roberts had meant by her reference to Meghan and Reverend Mullen.

"I got the distinct impression, Meghan, that Mrs. Roberts was being quite patronizing. Was she suggesting that you might not be a suitable person, should Reverend Mullen decide to favor a local woman with his attention?"

Conner bristled at the thought of another man, reverend or not, being interested in his Meghan. And the insinuation that she might be lacking, not good enough for the good reverend, was almost more than he could stand.

Mrs. Roberts was going too far. Perhaps it was time to show the good people of Pig Eye Gulch that Meghan O'Reiley no longer had to fight her battles alone. So deep was he in his thoughts that he almost missed Meghan's answer.

"I was hoping you didn't pick up on that, Holly." She gave a sigh he could hear through the walls of the shed. "Mrs. Roberts is of the opinion that, because of my questionable parentage, I am not of high value, shall we say, in the marriage market. As if I cared!" But the hurt in Meghan's voice cried out that she did care. She cared a great deal.

"And you, Meghan. What do you think?" Holly probed.

Conner knew he should move on. He knew it would be the honorable thing to do. The conversation was private between Meghan and his mother. It wasn't meant for him or anyone else to hear. But he couldn't move on, and he held his breath as he waited for Meghan's reply.

Her voice was low, almost inaudible. "I . . . I guess I agree with her."

"Oh, Meghan, my dear, you can't mean that."

"I know who and what I am, Holly. And it's not bad, so don't look so shocked at my answer. I'm Meghan O'Reiley. Plain Meghan O'Reiley."

Conner winced. Why did her words pierce his heart? Because, he reasoned, she believed them. And because, she believed them, she'd believe that there was no place for him in her life. Black night entered his heart. Who was he fooling? Meghan wouldn't let herself love him, no matter how patient he might be. He wasn't a quitter, but perhaps it was time to realize he was fighting a losing battle. It was apparent that Meghan didn't love him the way he loved her. If she did, parentage be darned, she wouldn't let anything stand in their path, would she? Finding no happy answer to that question, he turned and wearily walked away, the anticipated jaunt with Lady forgotten.

Later that afternoon, a clanging bell cut through the autumn stillness of the valley. The wind carried its hysterical peals to Meghan's cabin, where she and Holly were rolling out pie dough.

"Meghan, listen. What is that?"

Meghan stopped and wiped her hands on her apron, her body tensed. "It's the bell . . . the mine!" Her voice cracked. "It's the mine bell, Holly." She jerked her apron off and, throwing it on the nearest chair, ran toward the door.

"Meghan, Meghan, wait. I don't—"

Meghan paused, her hand on the door. "Holly, it's the mine bell. It only rings when there's been some sort of accident." Her voice rose, laced with panic. "I have to go. I'll be needed. Oh, dear God, please don't let it be a cave-in." Her prayer rose, saturated with fear and anxiety.

"I'm coming too," Holly stated decisively, dusting her hands on her dress, not noticing the streaks of flow they left. "You'll need help." She stopped. "Bonnie. I forgot Bonnie."

"Take her to Marybeth," Meghan ordered. "In her condition, Marybeth can't help us. If she's asked to look after Bonnie, it will make her feel like she's doing something." Meghan talked fast, not giving Holly a chance to answer before she was halfway out the door. "Holly, take Bonnie, and then come directly to the mine. Do you know how to get there?"

"Yes. Oh, Meghan, I just thought of something. Where's Conner? I haven't seen him since breakfast, have you? Harry?" Her voice rose. "Where's Harry?"

"Holly, don't imagine the worst. They're both okay. They have to be. We don't have time to stand here dreaming up horrors. We have to hurry. Meet me there." She slammed the door and was out of sight before Holly could respond.

Pig Eye Gulch's worst nightmare had come true. Meghan arrived to hear what she'd feared. Her prayer hadn't been answered. It was a cave-in. There was no word yet of how many men were trapped below the dirt and rock or how the accident had happened. All she knew was that it was at the site where they were digging a newer, deeper shaft and that the afternoon shift was somewhere in that horrifying rubble. She looked around, seeing women crying at what had been a mine entrance only a few short hours ago. A dark pall hung over the area. Children clung to mothers' skirts. Older children stood together as if to gain strength, as if to reassure themselves that father, brother, cousin, or friend wasn't trapped down there, starving for air or crushed beneath the giant rocks that had tumbled out of the belly of the earth.

The crowd moved aside as they recognized Meghan. By unspoken agreement, they knew she was the woman best able to help. Meghan tried not to let her fear show, but she knew that in this type of emergency, if she was all they had, the help was woefully inadequate. A doctor was needed. Near the entrance, she spotted Harry. He saw her too and moved quickly, grabbing her to him.

"Meghan!" His voice was choked with dust. "Conner is in there, helping to bring out a few of the miners who were working near the face. There are more." His voice cracked. "Many more."

"Conner!" Meghan cried, then caught herself. She couldn't do that. She couldn't think of him down there. She couldn't allow herself to give in to the screaming fear threatening to engulf her. He was underground. Would another cave-in occur? If the shaft was already weakened, anything could happen. *Not Conner*, she prayed, *not Conner.* Then, realizing how selfish she was being, she pulled herself up. She would be of no use if she allowed herself to fall apart now.

"Harry, we need a doctor. They'll be bringing up the injured soon. I can only do so much. We need help, Harry, and we need it quickly."

"A doctor," he said, focusing on what had happened and what might happen to his son, now down below the ground.

"Yes. The nearest one's in Lewistown. Oh, Lord, by

the time you ride there and get a doctor and then ride back, it may be too late for some of these men. Harry!" Meghan grabbed him by the lapels. "Harry, you've got to telegraph."

"Telegraph?" he asked dully, his mind grappling with the words.

"Yes." She gave him a shake, forcing him to focus and look at her.

"I . . . I'm sorry, Meghan. Tell me what to do, and, by darn, I'll do it."

"We need to telegraph Lewistown and get a doctor here. Immediately! You did it once, Harry. You can do it again."

"I did it with Conner's help," he said brokenly. "I don't know if I can do it by myself."

"You can. I'll help. Isn't there a handbook? There has to be a handbook in Conner's office. Hurry, Harry. We have to hurry!" She tugged the big man, his suit crumpled in her fists.

An hour passed, two. The ground was covered with litters of men in varying stages of pain and injury. Voices rent the air. Harry had successfully sent the telegram. A doctor was on his way.

Meghan and Holly and several of the other women were doing all they could for the injured. Meghan was needed everywhere at once. She showed Holly how to press a folded cloth firmly over a gaping wound to stanch the flow of blood. Returning a few minutes later with a bag of dried herbs, she sprinkled them directly on the wounds. The herbs would slow and thicken the blood. A man moaned in pain, but he was one of the luckier ones.

How many? How many more? That question ran non-stop through her head. And hand in glove with this litany was dark, ever-present worry about Conner. Men said they had seen him digging with shovel and hands, working beside them as they removed rock after rock to get to a man, and then, when he was free, to move on to yet another.

"He's workin' like a dervish, he is, ma'am," one miner told her as he gently laid his end of a litter down on the ground, heavy with yet another injured worker. "He's right beside us, that he is. Right there where the roof is the worst. The air's plumb bad down there, but he won't come out for a breather." The man departed, leaving his words to seep into her very soul.

She was bent over a miner, tearing pants away from a bloody leg that was surely broken, when she felt a tap on her shoulder. Looking up, she saw a clean face and kindly eyes looking intently at her. "Are you Meghan O'Reiley?"

"I am."

"I am Dr. Sinclair. Just arrived from Lewistown."

"Thank you, Lord," she whispered. "I've tended to the ones I knew I could give immediate help to, but there are others for whom I haven't the knowledge." She broke off, her voice filled with remorse at her limitations.

'Well, you've got help now, Miss O'Reiley. You can brief me on each man's condition as we go along. Looks like you've fought quite a battle," he said, his eyes full of admiration for the young woman with the dirt-streaked face.

"I . . . I've had help. But there are still men they are trying to get out."

Speaking only when needed to discuss a condition or to give instructions, the two went from man to man. Meghan worked tirelessly, following the doctor's orders, her hands knowing what to do without being told. Many the times he looked up at her with a nod and a smile of encouragement.

They were able to move the less severely injured to the large mess tent, where wives and more women from the valley cared for them. Those whose injuries were too severe lay unmoved.

Meghan arched her back and wiped a hand across her face. She had been working for hours, and still no sign of Conner. Harry had taken up vigil at the face of the mine and, from time to time, would report anything he heard.

He approached her now, and her heart froze at the look on his face.

"Conner?" she asked, her voice hoarse with a suppressed scream. "Harry, is it Conner?"

"Two men are trapped," he said. "There's a hole big enough to squeeze through. The roof's bad, threatening to cave in at any moment. Meghan, honey, one of the men trapped is Emery Phillips. We don't know if they're alive or not. Hope's not real high about either man's condition."

Meghan swayed. Harry reached for her, steadying

her for his next onslaught of news. "Conner's going in after them."

"No!" she cried. "No, he can't. Harry, you've got to stop him." Meghan agonized. Had she been wrong to keep Emery's secret? And were Emery and Conner about to pay for her mistake with their lives?

"Meghan, I can't stop. Conner. He's his own man. He'll feel responsible for this accident and the many injuries. I know I would if it were my mine. Now, you look at me." He gave her a shake. "He's going to be okay. He's refusing to let any other man take the risk. Meghan, look around you. The women here, the doctor—they are depending on you. And, honey, so is Conner."

She closed her eyes, and when she opened them she felt swamped by pain. "Harry, I've been selfish, thinking only of my fears, when I have Emery and Marybeth to think of. I've got to find Holly and send her to Marybeth. When she hears Emery is trapped," she said, "possibly dead, anything could happen. She and the baby could be at risk. Dear God, Emery, not Emery. He's so good, so . . ." She turned away, breaking Harry's grip as she squared her shoulders and lifted her chin. "I'll be here, Harry," she said softly, her voice strong. "Let me know the very minute you know anything. Anything!" She went back to the doctor's side, banishing the images and her fears to the darkest recesses of her mind.

Time had no value. It seemed only minutes later when a wave of sound swept over the area, reaching her. A sound filled with voices, a sound of doom and foreboding. Meghan froze, every fiber of her body still and listening. A miner came running toward her.

"Ma'am, I was told to tell you they're bringing the two men out." He glanced at the doctor, looking apprehensive. "One's dead, and the other's arm is hanging by a thread. He'll lose it for sure." The dire prediction had just crossed his lips when he added as an afterthought, "If he lives. Way he's bleeding"—he shook his head— "looks like a goner." He looked from one to the other.

"Do you know their names?" Meghan demanded.

"No, ma'am, I don't."

The words were no sooner out of his mouth when a group of men, two litters between them, came into sight. Meghan and the doctor rushed toward them. Meghan's one thought was to get a look at each man's face to see for herself Emery's fate.

Her first glance told her the dead man wasn't Emery. But before she could breathe a prayer of thanks, the men parted, and she saw the next man. Emery wasn't dead but close to it. The doctor ran to him and began applying a tourniquet to stanch the bleeding.

Meghan was just behind him when she heard someone say, "He's under the rubble. Another cave-in. I tried to talk him out of going down that hole. Well, he got these two out, but it's anyone's guess if we can get *him* out. And if we do, the chances don't look none too good he'll be breathin'."

The words hit Meghan like a giant fist, and her world as she knew it ceased to be. She stumbled over to the men, her feet as heavy as if mired in quicksand. "Is it . . . is it Mr. Hendrickson?" The words were torn from her.

A man nodded.

She bowed her head and, turning away from their inquisitive looks, took several deep breaths. Then she turned back, the brilliance of her eyes dulled with anguish. "Let me know immediately when you know anything at all about him. Do you understand? Immediately."

"Yes, ma'am, we surely will." The men moved off as one back toward the face of the mine and the one man left to be pulled from the earth's belly.

The doctor looked up at her approach. "I think we can save this one." He looked down at Emery. "We can't save the arm, but he's lucky they got him out when they did. Much longer and he would have bled to death.

"Not 'they,' Doctor," she mumbled. " 'They' didn't get him out. One man did. One man risked his life." Her voice broke. "Conner Hendrickson."

She didn't see the doctor's quizzical look. Through tear-filled eyes she saw only Emery and his chest rising with each breath.

It seemed an eternity as they worked on him. They transferred him to a litter for transport to the mess tent as soon as the doctor felt he was stable enough to withstand the jostling. Then she heard a shout. Turning toward the sound, she saw Harry running toward her.

"No," she said quietly. "Please no." And she steeled herself for the worst.

"He's out, Meghan!" he shouted. "They got him out."
He reached her, panting for breath, his smile wide.

"Meghan, they got him out. He's alive. He's unconscious—a rock hit him, and he's pretty cut up—but he's alive. He's the last, Meghan." He reached out and touched her. "He's alive, Meghan. Our Conner's alive."

Chapter Twenty-five

Night had fallen. The remaining men, including Conner, were in the mess tent. The doctor moved silently from one man to another, checking and watching. Three had died, but the rest were doing as well as could be expected, Conner and Emery among them.

Emery had regained consciousness and was able to tell them what had happened. Several of the new men had decided to have a race, double-jacking and setting the powder to see which group could sink the most feet in the shaft each day. Emery said the experienced miners tried to stop them but were outnumbered by a few hotheads. They had been racing for several shifts. Finally, seeing that their foolhardy actions weren't going to stop, Emery had planned to seek Conner out and inform him at the end of the shift. But he'd waited too long. One of the shots was set in a haphazard rush, and the result was now history.

"I owe him my life," Emery weakly told them. "I'd uh died down there, hadn't been for Mr. Hendrickson. I guess an arm is a small price to pay." His eyes beseeched Marybeth's for understanding. "I don't know what we'll do now, Marybeth, my girl. Not much demand for a one-armed miner. If only I'd acted sooner. Men lost, injured . . ." The sentence was left unfinished as his eyes closed and he drifted into a drug-induced sleep. Relief had taken its sweet time coming, dulling the pain that screamed through his body.

Marybeth wiped the tears from her eyes. The arm seemed a small price to pay. They had each other, and that was all that counted, she told Meghan. They had each other, and they had their babies. Somehow they would manage. She held Emery's one hand, her head bowed in thankfulness and in prayers for the women who had been less fortunate than she. And Meghan vowed to make good on her promise to look after his family if anything happened to him, even though, thank the Lord, he had survived.

Conner had yet to regain consciousness. The doctor had warned them it might be days Head injuries were tricky things, and so much about them was unknown. What he hadn't said, but what Meghan feared, was the chance that Conner might never regain consciousness. Meghan held his lifeless hand in hers. She would not, could not, consider that possibility.

She looked into the bruised face of the man she loved,

the man she had almost lost that afternoon. She left his side only when the doctor needed her assistance. Holly had offered to spell her, but she had refused. She couldn't bear the thought of not being there should he need her, should he waken.

Thoughts whirled through her head, thoughts of things she had said to him and things she hadn't said. Things she prayed she'd have the opportunity to rectify. Numbness swept her, and she shifted her position.

She glanced over at her friend Marybeth. Holly and Harry were spending the night at their cabin, looking after Jimmy and Bonnie, leaving Marybeth to be with Emery. Theirs was a love worth envying. Like the love she hoped to have with Conner, if she wasn't too late. If he still wanted her. If . . . She refused to acknowledge the other *if*'s.

She saw Marybeth grimace and rub a hand across her stomach. Then she placed the other hand in the small of her back and took a deep breath.

Meghan watched with sudden realization. She quietly rose and went to her friend. "Marybeth, you're having contractions, aren't you?"

Marybeth nodded. "Yes, but I don't want to leave him," Meghan," she whispered. She looked imploringly at Meghan. "I almost lost him. Had it not been for Mr. Hendrickson, Jimmy and this baby would have no father. But, Meghan . . ." She reached out and took Meghan's hand, squeezing it. "He'll regain consciousness. I know he will." Her face tightened with the last words, and she gripped her friend's hand harder as another labor pain hit her.

"Marybeth, how long have you been having pains?"

"Since early afternoon, just before the cave-in."

"Oh, Marybeth," she said, "and you didn't say anything?"

"Meghan, don't scold me. I was going to send for you, but . . . but then everything happened. Others needed you more than me. But"—she attempted to smile—"I think I need you now, and I think we'd better find as private a place as possible, as soon as possible, because I think you're about to deliver my daughter."

"I'll get the doctor." Meghan tried to release her hand.

"No! No doctor. You're the one I trust. You're the one I want to deliver my baby. But, Meghan, I don't think we have time to argue."

Marybeth was right. They didn't have time to argue. Meghan had no sooner set up a cot in the cookshack and settled Marybeth in it, when she gave birth to a beautiful baby girl. The doctor came by to assist if he was needed. He wasn't. It was an easy birth, and even though there had been a scramble to gather up the necessary items, the baby's lusty cry told them all was well.

The doctor kept a watchful eye on Conner and reported back often to Meghan. There was no change. The night seemed to be filled with extra hours. Meghan longed for morning and the dawning of a new, better day. Surely Conner would waken with the sun. Surely he would.

But he didn't. And two mornings later they moved him to her cabin. The jostling ride didn't seem to faze the sleeping man. His bruises were changing colors, and one side of his face was a deepening purple. Meghan called on every ounce of knowledge she had and, through her efforts, reduced the swelling. He was healing. On the outside. The doctor tried to reassure her, telling her that the sleep could be his body's way of healing. The physician seemed to find reassurance in Conner's occasional jerky movements, even though he hadn't yet opened his eyes or uttered a sound. Meghan took comfort from this and from the fact that he was resting under her roof, in her bed. She spent her nights curled up in a chair or, when Holly could coax her, on a pallet by the side of his bed.

Harry had taken over running the mine. The rubble was being cleared, and although the names of the miners responsible for the cave-in were known, no one was being punished. Everyone had suffered enough.

"Meghan, I'm worried about you," Holly said one morning after laying Bonnie down for a nap. "I insist you do something besides hover over Conner's bedside. Go outside. See the fall colors. The trees are beautiful shades of gold and orange. See the geese flying over. You can hear them honking as they fly by. Please, dear, the valley is putting on quite a show; take a few minutes to enjoy it."

Meghan got up and stretched wearily. "I can't, Holly. I can't leave him." She shook her head. "I let Conner down once. I can't let him down again."

"Meghan, I've tried not to pry, but perhaps I should. You're punishing yourself for something you think you've done. What is it? Perhaps sharing will help."

Meghan sighed, then reluctantly walked into the kitchen and sat down across from Holly. "I don't think anyone can help me but Conner. You see, Holly, I love him."

"I know you do, child. I know you do. But what I don't know is why that should be such a source of heartache for you."

"Because . . ." She faltered, then went on. "I never told him. I've led him to think just the opposite. I've led him to think there was no possibility of love between us."

"Why on earth would you do that? It's obvious to Harry and me how much Conner thinks of you. Has he neglected to tell you?"

"No. Oh, he hasn't said so in so many words." At his mother's frown, she hurried on to explain. "He tried, Holly. Right after he came back from Helena, he tried, but I stopped him."

Silence shared the space between them as Meghan gathered the words to continue. Holly waited patiently.

"He started to ask me to share his life. I know that's what he was going to do, but I told him we could only be friends."

"Why, Meghan? Why would you deny him your love?"

"Because I'm not like you, Holly. I'm not like the other women Conner has known."

"Well, thank the good Lord for that. But what do you mean, you aren't like me? Of course you are. We are both women of substance, and I don't mean money!"

Meghan looked up, puzzled by the words.

"Meghan, Bonnie's mother was not only shallow, she was conniving, only after his money. She didn't love Conner or her baby. Conner was too young, too trusting, to see her for what she was. Harry and I knew she'd hurt him, and she did. Hurt him so deeply, we had almost lost hope he'd ever love again. But that first day we arrived and he introduced you, we could see, by the way he looked at you and the pride in his voice, that he'd found someone worthy of the love he wanted to give. Someone who had healed him of all his hurt and anger. As we grew to know you, we could understand why. You are a remarkable woman, Meghan O'Reiley."

"But . . ." Meghan protested, the blue of her eyes clouded as she battled through the doubts, "I'm not sophisticated. I . . . I don't know my parents. I'm not . . ." She never got to finish the sentence.

A voice from the other room, a voice they had all been living to hear, interrupted. Weak as it was, it could be heard loud and clear. "You're everything a man could want."

"Conner!" they cried. One woman rushed to his bedside, the other one, a radiant smile of joy and thanksgiving on her face, stepped outside into the autumn day, a day made for living and rejoicing.

Meghan fell at his bedside, tears streaming down her face. She reached for his hand. "Conner, my beloved Conner, you're awake."

His smile was weak, but when their eyes met, the joy in his was strong. "I'm awake, and unless I'm dreaming, I just heard a beautiful woman call me 'beloved.'"

She blushed but didn't pull back. "Yes, I did. I have something to tell you, and it can't wait another minute. I should have told you this before, and I almost lost my chance. But I won't ever let that happen again, for I plan to tell you every day of my life, I love you, Conner Hendrickson. I love you."

He wiped a tear from her cheek, then tilted her face to his. "And I love you, Meghan O'Reiley. And I plan to tell *you* that every day of my life. I think I fell in love with you the first time I saw you, that fateful day I opened my door and found you holding Bonnie. That day you lit into me and let me know what you thought of a man who would leave a baby alone in a pen."

She blushed at the memory. "I was terrible, wasn't I?"

"No, you weren't terrible at all. You were fighting for my daughter, just like you've fought for everyone who needs you. Now, tell me my beloved, what do I have to do to convince you to marry me?"

"Ask me," she whispered. "Just ask me."

"Meghan O'Reiley, would you do me the honor, the amazing honor, of being my wife?"

He didn't need to hear her answer. Words didn't need to be spoken. Her eyes were eloquent as they glowed with a brilliance that would put the bluest sapphire to shame. For in her eyes shone all the love they would need to carry them through the years to come. A love as big as the mountains. A love as wide as her valley. A love worth more than all the sapphires in Conner's mine. A love that would never dim, shining forth from eyes of sapphire blue.

B